KIANA'S HERO

BROTHERHOOD PROTECTORS HAWAII
BOOK THREE

(

ELLE

TWISTED PAGE INC

KIANA'S HERO

BROTHERHOOD PROTECTORS HAWAII
BOOK #3

New York Times & *USA Today*
Bestselling Author

ELLE JAMES

ISBN EBOOK: 978-1-62695-546-2

ISBN PAPERBACK: 978-1-62695-547-9

Dedicated to my readers who make my dreams come true by keeping me in the business I love dearly...WRITING! I love you all so much. Thank you for buying my books!
Elle James

AUTHOR'S NOTE

Enjoy other military books by Elle James

Visit ellejames.com for more titles and release dates
Join her newsletter at
https://ellejames.com/contact/

CHAPTER 1

Kiana Williams leaned her head back against the thin seat of the commuter plane that would carry her and Devlin Mulhaney from the Hawaiian island of Maui to Oahu. Flight time was less than forty minutes from wheels up to wheels down. She closed her eyes in an attempt to discourage conversation with the man. "Thank you for being on time to catch our flight this morning."

"My pleasure," he said, his tone low, sexy and too much for that early.

A shiver of awareness rippled across her skin.

"Since I'm here to protect you and, potentially, your friend, you should bring me up to speed on her—where she lives, what she does for a living, and anything else I might need to know."

Kiana's lips pressed into a thin line. "You're

supposed to be the expert protector. I would think you could react to any situation."

He chuckled. "I'm not a mind-reader. As a former Marine Force Reconnaissance operator, I am combat trained; however, you can never have too much information about your opponent or the situation. We never went in blind unless we absolutely had no other choice."

She sighed. "Fair enough." Without lifting her head, she told him what she knew, which wasn't much. She'd been up through the night worried about her friend and former roommate, trying to guess what could have happened. Every potential scenario she came up with was increasingly horrible, giving her a bad feeling in the pit of her belly.

Kiana opened her eyes and sat up straight. "My friend and former roommate, Meredith O'Neil, shares an apartment with my other friend, Tish Brinks. As you know, Tish called yesterday to say Meredith was missing." Dev had been there when she'd gotten the call. "Normally, I wouldn't be too worried. Meredith has been known to stay a night or two with her boyfriend. When Tish clarified Meredith had been gone for a week, that was different. Staying over with a boyfriend for a night or two was one thing; not coming home for a week is another."

"Did Tish try calling Meredith's boyfriend?" Dev asked.

Kiana grimaced. "Tish said Meredith had broken up with her boyfriend over a month ago. He's out of the picture."

"Still worth a call," Dev pointed out. "They could've gotten back together."

Kiana nodded. "Tish called. No answer. The last she'd heard from Meredith was that she was taking an escort job to help make rent money. Apparently, that was the night she disappeared, as far as Tish could tell. Meredith hadn't texted to say she was staying the night with a friend, a man or anyone else."

Dev frowned. "An escort job? What do you mean?"

Kiana glanced at Dev, her brow wrinkling. "It's like going on a date with someone, only you get paid."

"That could be dicey," Dev said.

Kiana's brow dipped. "It's not prostitution.

Dev gave her half a smile. "I didn't say it was."

Kiana had the sudden urge to defend her friend and the profession of paid escorts. "Usually, it's a businessman wanting someone to attend a corporate function with him, or a wealthy man who just wants someone to eat dinner with him, rather than sitting at a table by himself."

"Do the clients expect more?"

"Some do," Kiana admitted. "Before an escort is assigned, the escort service explains the rules and emphasizes the service isn't for sex. It's up to the escort to state upfront about what she expects and her limits to reinforce what the service already told them."

Dev met and held her gaze. "How often does the client push for more?"

Kiana looked away. "If the escort states the ground rules, the client usually abides by them."

"What percentage of the time?" he persisted.

Kiana's gut clenched. "About fifty percent of the time."

"And you know this because…" he asked, his voice quiet, carrying only to her over the roar of the jet engines.

Kiana's lips curled into a tight smile as she turned to meet his gaze. "I used to work as an escort. When modeling jobs weren't plentiful, we had to make money for food, gas and rent." She lifted her chin, daring him to make a disparaging comment about being an escort. "And no. I didn't sleep with the clients. Yes, I had to fight off a few."

Dev's eyebrows dipped low. "Assholes."

She let out a short bark of laughter. "You have no idea."

He reached for her hand and gave it a quick squeeze before releasing it. "Why did Tish wait so long to call you?"

"Tish was on a modeling gig on Kauai for a couple of days and assumed Meredith had made it back from her escort assignment." Kiana's lips twisted.

"Based on the backlog of mail overflowing their mailbox and mold growing on the half-eaten bowl of cereal in the sink, Tish realized Meredith probably hadn't been back since her last message."

"Did she call the escort service?" Dev asked.

Kiana nodded. "They said they'd check into it but never got back to Tish."

"What about the police?"

"She called the police and reported Meredith as missing. I talked to Tish again last night after the police came to the apartment to ask questions. They said they'd follow up with the escort service and check in with the ex-boyfriend." Kiana wrapped her arms around her middle as a chill rippled across her body. "Tish is beside herself. She feels awful that Meredith could've been missing for a whole week, and no one has been looking for her. Don't they say the first forty-eight hours are the most important?"

Dev nodded. "Yeah. The first forty-eight hours after a crime has been committed is like the sweet spot for gathering evidence. After that, it gets harder to locate clues. They could be destroyed or thrown out with the trash. Finding people who might've seen something important to a case gets trickier."

"And memories fade the further away from the event you get." Kiana sighed. "That's what I'm afraid of."

"Why not leave it to the police to investigate?"

Dev asked. "They should have better access to information."

Kiana snorted softly. "And how many crimes are they investigating every day? A missing woman who worked as an escort might not rank high enough on their leader board, or whatever they call it." Her eyes narrowed. "The escort service might not be as open to the police with confidential client information. They'll likely wait for a search warrant."

"Which will take time to acquire." Dev's lips pressed together into a thin line.

Kiana nodded. "Time Meredith might not have. Plus, I figure the more people looking for her, the sooner we find her."

"Good point, and I'm here to help," Dev said. "We should exchange phone numbers in the unlikely event we're separated." He offered her his cell phone and held out his empty hand for hers.

Her brow furrowed as she clutched her phone to her chest.

His eyebrows rose in challenge. "It's not like I'm going to call you for a date. You made that very clear."

As she laid her phone in his palm, her fingers brushed against his skin, sending a spark of electricity shooting up her arm that shocked her in more ways than one. She grabbed his phone and quickly entered her number into his contact list, reminding herself he was her bodyguard.

Exchanging numbers was expected. Still, it felt strangely…intimate.

Once they had their own phones back, Dev slipped his into his pocket and glanced at her. "So, what's the plan?"

"First stop is the apartment. Tish might've heard back from the escort service. If she hasn't, we'll go there next." Kiana adjusted her seatbelt as the plane descended into the Honolulu International Airport.

While the plane taxied across the tarmac, Kiana called Tish.

"Are you here?" Tish answered on the first ring.

"I am." Kiana tensed at the worry in her friend's tone. "We just landed. I'll be there in less than half an hour."

"Oh, thank God," Tish said. "I don't know what else to do."

"It'll be okay," Kiana said. "We'll find her."

"I hope so," Tish said. "Hurry."

"I will." Kiana ended the call as the plane rolled to a stop. She grabbed her backpack from beneath the seat and followed Dev out.

Once in the open-air terminal, she pulled out her cell phone to arrange a lift.

Before she could request a pickup, Dev covered her hand. "I called ahead for a rental car. I figured we'd need to get around on our own without waiting for a taxi or ride-share. They'll have the keys ready. All we have to do is grab the keys and go."

Kiana's brow dipped. "You did that?"

"I did. Come on." He took her hand and led her through the airport to the rental car agency. All he had to do was give his name, and they handed over a set of keys and gave him directions to the vehicle.

Moments later, Kiana slid into the passenger seat, relieved she didn't have to wait for a ride and didn't have to do the driving in the heavy Honolulu traffic. As much as she didn't like relying on a man for anything, she was glad she had Dev with her. There was no room for stubborn independence as long as her friend was missing. She'd take all the help she could get.

And if he was handsome as hell, it wouldn't hurt to look. As long as she didn't do something stupid like fall for the guy.

She shook her head. Not a chance. Kiana had learned her lesson the hard way.

Never fall for the cute guy. He'd lie, steal your money and break your heart. Having been burned once, she refused to get that close to another flame.

"WHERE ARE WE GOING?" Dev asked as he familiarized himself with the car's controls and started the engine.

Kiana entered an address on her smartphone and hit Go.

Between the voice on the phone and Kiana, he

was able to leave the airport and merge into the traffic heading toward Waikiki.

Kiana leaned forward in her seat, her brow knitted, one hand clenching her cell phone and the other digging into the armrest on the door.

Dev couldn't ease her worry with words. The only thing that would help would be to find her friend Meredith waiting at the apartment when they arrived. Kiana's conversation with Tish hadn't been promising. The sooner they got there, the sooner they could get started on their quest to find the missing roommate.

They left the airport, merged onto Highway 1, and soon left the highway to wind through the streets of Honolulu.

After the sixth turn, Dev slowed. "Where from here?"

Kiana laid a hand on his arm. "Stop."

Dev pressed a foot to the brake in front of a small apartment building a couple of blocks from a major road.

"Park at the rear of the building," Kiana said. "The apartment is in the back."

Dev drove around to the back of the building and found a parking space in the far corner next to a large trash bin. As soon as he shifted into Park, Kiana unclipped her seatbelt and shoved open her door.

He reached out and touched her arm. "I'm here to protect you," he said. "Let me."

She met his gaze and nodded. "Okay."

He quickly released his seatbelt and slid out of the driver's seat.

Kiana met him at the rear of the vehicle. She nodded toward the three-story building. "The apartment is on the second floor."

He took her hand, led her up the exterior metal stairs to the second floor and walked along the landing until Kiana stopped in front of the door marked 216. When she raised her hand to knock, Dev caught her arm and shook his head.

She frowned.

He touched a finger to his lips and dipped his chin toward the door, stepping between her and the knob.

The door stood ajar by barely an inch.

Kiana's eyes widened, and she stepped back behind Dev.

Stay here, he mouthed.

She nodded.

Dev pushed the door open, wishing he had an M4A1 rifle like he'd carried into urban battle in places like Iraq and Afghanistan. Either that or a handgun.

As a civilian, having just gotten off an airplane and working a bodyguard-for-hire job on the island of Oahu, he was unarmed and unprepared for a major battle. All he had to rely on was his wits. No gun, no knife. Just his hands and years of experience.

The lights were off inside the apartment, which

worked for Dev and for anyone who might be lurking inside.

He eased open the door, inch by inch. Once it was wide enough for a full-grown man to enter, he hunkered low, slipped through the gap and stepped out of the wedge of light shining through behind him. Assuming a ready stance, he let his eyes adjust to the dark interior and strained to hear sounds of movement.

A pitiful feminine moan sounded from deeper inside the apartment, muffled by a wall or door. "Please…don't…I'm…not…her."

Every instinct on alert, Dev rushed toward the sound.

"No? Then where is she?" a deep, harsh voice demanded. Something loud crashed in another room.

Dev rounded a corner and raced down a short hallway with a bathroom at the end and a door on either side. The door on the right was open, the room in shambles.

A loud thud sounded as if something heavy hit the wall in the room on the left. "Tell me!" a man shouted.

Dev reached for the handle of the closed door and tried to turn it. It was locked.

"Tell me!" the man screamed. Another thud made the wall shake.

Kiana appeared beside Dev. "Oh my God. Tish?" She pounded her fist against the door.

Suspecting the man was hurting the woman, Dev grabbed Kiana and moved her away from the door. He backed far enough away and then kicked as close to the doorknob as he could.

The door frame cracked but held.

On his second kick, the frame split, and the door slammed open.

Nothing moved in the room except a filmy curtain hanging beside an open window.

A dark-haired woman lay crumpled against the wall, unmoving.

Kiana squeezed past Dev and dropped to her knees beside the woman. "Tish." She felt for a pulse. "Tish, sweetie, it's me, Kiana." Tears streamed down her cheeks. "I feel a pulse," she said. "I'm calling 911." She looked up at Dev. "Don't let him get away."

"What if he comes back?" Dev asked.

"I'm calling 911. We can't let him get away. Not after what he's done to Tish." She waved toward the window. "Either you go after him, or I will. Go!"

Dev raced for the open window and stared out.

Footsteps pounded against the landing. A man dressed in black with a black ball cap ran toward the end of the landing.

With no time to backtrack through the apartment, Dev pulled himself through the window and hit the landing running.

By that time, the assailant had reached the end of the building only to realize he'd passed the staircase leading to ground level. He turned, saw Dev heading his way and vaulted over the wrought-iron railing, dropping to the ground below.

He hit hard, rolled and staggered to his feet.

Dev didn't wait to get to the end of the landing, he braced his hands on the railing and launched himself over. When he hit the ground, he tucked and rolled as he'd learned during parachute jump school. He was on his feet in seconds, racing after the man several yards ahead of him.

The attacker moved with a decided limp, ducking through an alley and between buildings.

Dev was faster, quickly closing the distance between them.

When Dev was only two yards from catching the man, the assailant burst out of the densely packed buildings. He crossed a sidewalk, dodged between a couple of parked cars and raced out into a four-lane road.

A horn blared, tires squealed, and a huge garbage truck slammed into the man in black. The impact knocked him to the ground. The truck's front tire bumped over him before the vehicle rolled to a stop.

Dev had made it to the parked cars when he heard the horn. He was able to arrest his forward progress short of running out in front of another car. Too late to stop the inevitable, he waited until all traffic came to a complete halt.

When he was certain he wasn't going to be the

next person run over, he ran to the body lying on the pavement between the front and back axles of the garbage truck and knelt beside him to feel through the man's pockets for a wallet or some form of identification. His pockets were empty but for a packet of cigarettes. It wouldn't do any good to take a photo of the guy with his head crushed.

Dev pushed the man's right sleeve up, searching for any kind of identifying marks. Nothing. When he pushed the left sleeve up, he found a Polynesian mask inked in black on the inside of the man's forearm. He quickly snapped a photo of the tattoo with his cell phone.

The truck driver dropped out of the driver's seat. "I couldn't stop," he said, his voice shaking. "Is he...?"

"Dead?" Dev nodded. He didn't have to feel for a pulse. The garbage truck's wheel had rolled over the man's skull, crushing it beneath its massive weight.

"Sweet Jesus," the truck driver muttered, fumbling in his pocket. "We need to call 911."

Another man approached, his cell phone pressed to his ear. "I just placed a call to 911. They're sending someone now."

The truck driver quit digging for his phone and ran his hand through his dark hair. "I've never run over a man before. Did you know him? Was he a friend?"

Dev straightened, shaking his head. "No. I don't know him. And no, he wasn't a friend. He assaulted a woman. Excuse me." He stepped away from the truck, the driver and the good Samaritan reporting the accident.

"Sir, you're not leaving, are you?" the truck driver called out.

"Not yet," Dev responded.

"Good, 'cause you're the main witness." The distraught garbageman stared down at the dead man, frowning worriedly. "The police are going to want to talk to you."

"I need to check on the woman this guy attacked." He hadn't wanted to leave Kiana alone. Now that Tish's attacker was neutralized, he was anxious to get back to the women. This man was dead, but that didn't mean he was the only one who could hurt Kiana and Tish.

After Kiana's phone rang three times, Dev was getting worried.

"Dev," she finally answered. "Where are you? Are you all right? Did you catch him?"

He was so relieved to hear her voice that he had to take a breath before answering, "I'm several blocks away from the apartment building. I'm all right, but Tish's attacker isn't. How's Tish?"

"I'm worried about her. She's nonresponsive. The paramedics are working with her now, loading her into an ambulance. I'm going to ride with her to the hospital. What do you mean the attacker isn't all right?"

"He's dead."

"Holy shit," Kiana murmured. "Did you…"

Dev shook his head, his lips quirking on the corners. "No. I didn't kill him. He ran out into a busy street and was hit by a garbage truck."

"Oh, thank God," Kiana said. "The bastard deserved to die."

"Yeah," he agreed. "Only it's too bad we couldn't question him first."

"Do you know who he is?" she asked. "Was there any form of identification on him?"

"I felt in his pockets," Dev said. "He wasn't carrying an ID."

"Okay, I'm coming." Kiana's voice sounded distant, as if she was talking to someone else away from her phone. Then she came back to him with, "Look, the ambulance is getting ready to leave. I have to go."

Dev's gut knotted. If she left the apartment, she'd be even further away from him than she was at that moment. "Are you going to be all right?" he asked. "I'll have to stay and talk with the police."

"I'll be okay. Police are crawling all over the apartment. I'll be safe in the ambulance. Can you meet me at the Queens Medical Center when you free up?"

"I will. And Kiana, stay with people," Dev said. "We don't know if this man was working for someone else. He attacked Tish. Whoever sent him might come after you next."

"I'll be okay until you get to me," she said. "Just hurry." The call ended.

Dev stared down at the phone, wishing he could go to Kiana immediately.

He had a really bad feeling in his gut about what had just happened.

Through all the years he'd spent on active duty and all the missions he'd been involved with, his gut feelings had never been wrong.

CHAPTER 2

IN THE BACK of the ambulance, Kiana sat on a bench across from Tish, her heart pinching hard in her chest.

Her friend and former roommate hadn't regained consciousness. Her face was bruised, her lip split and a gash over her left eye had left a trail of blood across her temple to mat in her dark hair.

The paramedics had done all they could to stabilize Tish for transport to the hospital. They'd set up an IV and connected a heart monitor to her chest.

The steady beep of the monitor was the only reassuring sound in the ambulance. As long as her heart was still beating, she had a chance.

Why didn't she wake up?

At the hospital, Tish was taken straight back to an examination room. A nurse stepped in front of Kiana when she tried to follow. "Are you a relative of the patient?"

"Her name's Tish Jenkins," Kiana said. "I'm the only relative she has. Tish and I grew up in the foster system together."

The nurse frowned. "No parents? Siblings? Spouse?"

"No." Kiana looked over her shoulder at the gurney disappearing with her friend on it. "Please. Tish was attacked and nearly killed. I'm her roommate, her sister of the heart. She hasn't regained consciousness since the attack and can't speak for herself. She needs someone to advocate for her. All she has is me."

The nurse's eyes narrowed, and she chewed on her bottom lip. Finally, she gave a curt nod. "Since you're her sister, you can go with her," she said and stepped aside.

Kiana hurried after Tish, catching up as the orderly pushed the gurney into an examination room.

Moments later, a doctor appeared. As he shined a light into Tish's eyes, he asked questions about what had happened. Kiana answered to the best of her knowledge. He performed a preliminary examination, noting injuries to her face, ribs, arms and everywhere that could be seen on the outside.

The more bruises and cuts he discovered, the deeper Kiana's heart sank into her belly.

All that time, Tish remained unconscious.

When the doctor had completed his examination, he turned to Kiana. "We'll perform a CT scan looking for injuries to her brain and run other tests. You can wait in the waiting room. Someone will let you know when you can see her again." He turned to the nurse, gave her instructions and then stepped toward the door.

"She's going to be all right, isn't she?" Kiana called out. "She's going to wake up, right?"

The doctor looked back and gave Kiana a gentle smile. "Head trauma can be tricky. We need to see what's happening and make decisions based on what we find. We'll do our best to help her."

Kiana nodded even as the doctor left the room.

The nurse opened the door wide and tipped her head toward the exit that led out of the emergency department. "You can wait in the lobby. I'm taking Ms. Jenkins for that CT scan. We'll let you know more as we get results."

"Thank you." Kiana stepped out of the room and waited in the wide hallway until the nurse pushed the gurney out of the room and disappeared through another door at the opposite end of the hall from the direction of the lobby.

Kiana pressed a hand to her chest, trying to ease the ache. Tish and Meredith were her sisters. They'd found each other in the foster care system and forged a bond that had carried through to adulthood. Kiana might still be living with Tish and Meredith if she hadn't had such a shitty breakup with her fiancé and opted to get the hell off Oahu.

She'd left to get away from Carl Brandon, former model and Kiana's ex-fiancé; the man who'd siphoned off every last cent of her savings for a downpayment on a Corvette convertible he'd had to have for his transition to real estate broker.

He'd passed his brokerage training with her help, and no sooner had he signed on with a large brokerage firm than he'd called off their engagement and walked away from their three-year relationship with the Corvette Kiana's savings had helped him buy.

Kiana had saved every dime she could of her next three paychecks from modeling gigs, packed what she could carry in her suitcase, gave everything else to Tish and Meredith and moved to Maui. That had been over a year ago, and she hadn't been back to Oahu since.

Until now.

But she'd stayed in touch with Tish and Meredith and had sent money when they were in a tight place financially, or she had extra. She'd tried to get them to move to Maui with her, but there were few jobs for models on the island. After the fires, there were even fewer jobs on Maui. So many people who'd lost their homes and places of employment had been displaced from Maui to other islands. It was just as well Tish and Meredith had stayed on Oahu.

Though Kiana had made new friends, she'd missed her sisters.

Kiana paced the length of the waiting room for the next forty-five minutes, waiting for Dev, waiting for news about Tish and going through everything she knew so far, which wasn't much. How was she supposed to be with Tish and look for Meredith at the same time?

She pulled out her cell phone and called Cliff Rey, manager of Aloha Escorts. When he didn't answer his personal number, she tried the escort service's business number. An automated response answered in a sexy female voice, "Need a date to make your Hawaiian stay complete? You can count on Aloha Escorts. Please leave your name, number and preferences, and we'll get right back with you."

Kiana frowned. When had they gone to voicemail instead of having a real person fielding calls? She hesitated to leave a message but had no other choice. "Cliff, it's Kiana. Call me as soon as you receive this message. You have my number. It's important. Life or death."

When she ended the call, she turned to see Dev enter the ER waiting room. He stopped inside the door and swept the room with his gaze. When it landed on her, his lips curled into a muted smile.

In seconds, he crossed the room, opened his arms and she fell into them.

Hell, she barely knew this man, but she felt instinctively safe with him. She didn't realize she was crying until he leaned back and tipped up her chin.

"Hey, why the tears?" His brow dipped low. "Tish?"

Kiana shook her head. "I don't know. They took her back for a CT scan and other tests a while ago. No one's come out to tell me anything yet."

"Did she wake up?"

More tears filled Kiana's eyes. "No."

"Let's ask." He slipped an arm around her waist and walked with her to the reception desk.

At that moment, the doctor emerged from the door marked authorized personnel only. When he spotted Kiana, he headed straight for her.

Dev's arm tightened around her waist, and he pulled her gently against him.

Kiana leaned into him, dreading what the doctor might say.

"The CT scan showed us what we expected. Ms. Jenkins has bleeding on the brain."

All the air left Kiana's lungs, and a humming sound filled her ears, muffling the doctor's next words.

"We consulted with the neurosurgeon on call. He wants to monitor her for now. If the swelling worsens, he'll have to perform surgery to relieve the swelling. We'll keep a close watch over her in intensive care and keep her blood pressure down."

"Has she woken up?" Kiana asked, already knowing the answer.

The doctor shook his head.

"Any idea when she might regain consciousness?" Again, Kiana knew his answer but had to ask.

"No. She could be out until the swelling goes down, or she could be in a coma for days or months." The doctor grimaced. "There's no way to predict with head trauma. She's being moved to a room. As soon as she's settled, they'll let you know. Visiting hours are limited, but she'll have the finest care."

"Thank you," Kiana said softly.

When the doctor left them, Kiana turned and buried her face against Dev's chest.

Both of his arms came up around her, holding her close. "She's going to be okay," he assured her.

"How do you know?" Kiana asked into his shirt. "Even the doctor can't promise anything."

He tipped her chin up. "Is she anything like you?"

Kiana sniffed. "Like me?"

"Yeah," he said with a smile, "strong, independent." He brushed a strand of Kiana's hair back behind her ear. "A fighter."

Her brow knitted. "She's pretty badass. But how can she fight against a brain bleed?"

"Fighters always manage," he said and pressed a kiss to Kiana's forehead.

"Dev!" a deep voice called out behind Kiana.

Dev looked over the top of her head and grinned. "Oh, good. He got here quick."

"Who?" Kiana spun to see a familiar face.

"You remember Reid Bennet?" Dev held out a hand to his friend. "Glad you made it so fast."

"We left Maui about the same time as you did in a boat. Hawk sent supplies from the big island to Maui. They arrived a few minutes after your plane left this morning. Angel and I escorted them here, courtesy of one of Leilani's tour boats. Hawk figured you might need some of the items in your search for Ms. O'Neal."

Dev tilted his head and cocked an eyebrow at his teammate. "If by supplies, you mean what I think you mean…"

Reid met Dev's gaze and nodded.

Dev's lips pressed into a tight line. "I could have used those supplies an hour ago."

"Sorry," Reid said. "We got them here as quickly as possible."

Kiana looked from Reid to Dev. "What are you talking about?"

Dev smiled down at her. "I'll fill you in later. Right now, shouldn't we go see your friend Tish?"

Kiana nodded. "I'd like that."

Dev glanced at Reid.

"I'm going with you," Reid said.

"Good." Dev touched a hand to the small of Kiana's back. "Do you know where they took Tish?"

Kiana shook her head.

Dev steered her toward the reception desk, where he turned a panty-melting smile on the poor woman manning the phone there. "Could you tell me where they took Tish Jenkins?"

The middle-aged woman's cheeks flushed bright pink. "Yes, sir. Of course."

Dev leaned over the counter and flashed her a mega-watt grin. "Your name is Janice?"

She nodded.

"Janice is a lovely name for a lovely lady."

The woman's fingers fumbled over the keyboard. "Thank you. I'll just...find...Ms. Jenkins." Her voice was breathy, as if she couldn't quite get enough air to her lungs.

Kiana understood exactly how the poor woman felt.

The entire time Dev aimed his charisma at the receptionist, Kiana reacted to his words, smile and hunkiness with equally embarrassing heat in her cheeks and core.

Damn the man.

He could charm the panties off a virgin.

"Thank you, Janice," Dev said.

The receptionist's fingers stumbled some more across the keyboard and then stopped. "There," she said with a smile. "She's been moved to the ICU."

Janice glanced up. "And you're in luck. It's visiting hour." She stared up into Dev's eyes and batted her lashes. "Is there anything else I can help you with?"

Dev shook his head. "You've done more than enough, Janice. Thank you." With one last smile at the besotted woman, Dev turned toward Kiana. "Shall we go see your friend?"

Oh, so now he remembered she'd been standing beside him the entire time as he'd flirted with the woman behind the counter.

Kiana frowned. "Are you sure you don't want to stay and talk some more with Janice?"

He cast a smooth grin at the receptionist. "I don't want to take up too much of her time."

"Oh, you're not taking up too much of my time," Janice insisted.

Kiana hooked his arm. "Oh, yes, he is. Come on, honey, we need to see Tish and get back to those errands we need to accomplish. Isn't that right, dear?"

Dev chuckled. "Absolutely, sweetheart. Lead the way."

Kiana, Dev and Reid entered the elevator and rode it up to the ICU floor.

"You really should dial back on the charm," Reid said. "You had poor Janice so flustered, she could barely manage the keyboard."

Kiana's lips pressed together to keep her from agreeing aloud with Reid. She shouldn't care about who Dev flirted with. Theirs was a purely business arrangement.

But man, if he'd turned that smile on Kiana, she'd have chucked the business part of their relationship out the window in a heartbeat.

She stood beside him close enough to feel the heat of his body and only wanted to get closer.

Her body was urging her in that direction while her mind was screaming *DANGER.*

Hadn't she learned her lesson already?

The door opened on the ICU floor. Kiana hurriedly stepped out and away from Dev, heading for the nurses' station.

As she waited for a nurse to finish keying something into her computer, Kiana glanced around at the rooms within sight of the station. A young, thin janitor, wearing a coverall jumpsuit and baseball cap with the hospital logo on it, stepped out of one of the rooms, pushing a plastic trashcan on wheels. He passed by Kiana with his head tipped low, his ball cap shading most of his face except for the lower half. He had a dark mustache and goatee and wore blue rubber gloves on his hands.

Kiana frowned as he passed her, pushing the trash container.

"Thank you for your patience," the nurse at the station said. "How can I help you?"

"We're looking for Tish Jenkins," Dev said to the nurse.

The nurse tipped her head toward the door the janitor had just exited.

Kiana's heart skipped several beats. When she turned to see where the janitor had gone, he was on the elevator, the doors closing in front of him.

The garbage can on wheels was parked to one side of the elevator.

Odd.

Kiana wasn't sure why she had a bad feeling. "Do the janitors typically leave trash bins next to the elevators?

The nurse glanced toward the elevator and frowned. "Not usually. I'll have someone move it."

Kiana met Dev's gaze. At the same moment, they turned and darted for the room the janitor had just left. The one Tish had been moved to.

Inside, the lighting was muted.

Kiana ran to the bed and stared down at Tish, then up at the heart monitor, measuring every beat of her friend's heart.

Kiana's pulse was racing faster than the beeps and didn't subside until she was certain nothing was amiss.

"What was that all about?" Reid asked from behind them.

"Maybe nothing," Kiana said, feeling foolish for where her thoughts had jumped. "It's just that the janitor had come out of Tish's room. Call me paranoid, but I thought he might not have been a janitor and might have come to harm Tish." She grimaced. "I'm a little punchy."

Dev toed a small trash can with his boot. "If he was a janitor, he didn't bother to collect any trash while he was in this room."

Kiana looked down at the items a nurse might have discarded while getting Tish settled. "Maybe he decided, because she was in a coma, she wasn't going to talk, anyway."

"Is she all right?" Reid asked, coming to stand beside Kiana.

"As far as I can tell, but then I'm not a doctor. Her heartbeat is steady. That's reassuring."

"What would a janitor be doing in the room with Tish if he wasn't collecting trash?" Dev asked.

"Good question," Kiana said, her brow furrowing. "I'm worried about leaving her, but I need to be looking for Meredith. After what happened to Tish, I can only imagine the worst could have happened to Meredith."

"I'll stay with Tish," Reid said.

"They have strict visiting hours," Kiana pointed out.

Reid shook his head. "This woman was brutally attacked. I'm sure I can get them to bend the rules for her bodyguard."

Kiana stroked Tish's arm. It felt so cool, and her face was pale. Because they'd intubated her, she was getting the air she needed, and her heart was beating steadily.

"I need to be two people," Kiana whispered. "One to stay with Tish, the other to look for Meredith."

"We could stay here and let Reid look for Meredith," Dev suggested.

Kiana shook her head and met Dev's gaze. "I need to be the one asking the questions. Some of the people we worked with won't talk to you if they don't know you." She frowned. "As it is, they might not talk to me if I have a man tagging along."

Dev's eyes narrowed. "I signed onto the mission to protect you. I can't do my job if I'm not with you at all times."

"As much as I value my independence and hate to admit it, I kind of like having you around." Kiana stared hard at him. "We'll have to come up with a good cover for you."

"You can tell people I'm your boyfriend," Dev offered.

Despite her past experience with Carl, a flutter of butterfly wings beat against Kiana's insides. "No. Boyfriends come and go. Some can't be trusted." Her lips curled up on the corners. "You need to be a colleague I'm mentoring. Someone who could potentially work with the escort service, talent agency, or both."

Dev blinked. "An escort?"

Kiana cocked an eyebrow. "What? It's okay for a

woman but not a man? Are you afraid you might be molested?"

"No." Dev held up a hand. "I guess I never considered being an escort or a model. I'm not sure I can pull it off."

Reid chuckled. "You've got the looks and know how to charm women."

"Reid's right," Kiana said. "If I'm showing you the ropes, it would be natural for you to be clueless about the two businesses. Thus, my reason for showing you the ropes."

Dev shrugged. "I'm game for anything that gets me in the door with you."

Kiana gave a brief nod. "Then you're my protégé. I found you on Maui and think you'll be a good fit for modeling and the escort business. How do you feel about modeling men's underwear?"

Dev's eyebrows rose. "Seriously?"

Kiana fought hard to keep from grinning. "Models take whatever jobs they can get, whether it's for underwear or perfume."

Reid snorted. "Some of those cologne ads are pretty spicy. You'd be lucky if you got to wear underwear in one of those."

Dev's eyebrows dipped low. "It's not like I'll get hired that quickly. I'm the new guy trying to break in. And I'm only playing the part until we find Meredith."

"True." Kiana's lips curled. "But I was thinking

about your potential interview with the escort agency."

"You're joking, right?" Dev frowned.

She cocked an eyebrow. "Am I?"

Reid laughed.

It was all Kiana could do to keep from laughing at the appalled expression on Dev's face.

Dev squared his shoulders and lifted his chin. "I'll dance naked, wearing bells on my toes, if it gets me in with you. Whatever it takes."

Kiana's breath lodged in her throat at the sudden image she had of Dev dancing naked in front of her. Heat rose up her neck into her cheeks.

Her little attempt at teasing to make Dev uncomfortable had completely backfired.

CHAPTER 3

CAUGHT off guard at the thought of parading around in his underwear, Dev was glad he'd turned his response around the way he had. The flush of color staining Kiana's cheeks was worth his bold promise.

Kiana spun away, returning her attention to her friend lying motionless on the hospital bed. "I want to stay and be here when Tish wakes. I imagine she'll be scared, not knowing how she got here."

"On a positive note, she might not remember the attack," Dev offered, crossing the room to stand beside Kiana.

"What if she doesn't remember anything at all?" Kiana whispered. "She'll have a long road of recovery ahead of her."

Dev knew of guys with traumatic brain injuries who'd lost their memories. Some had had to start over learning how to walk, talk, and feed themselves. He hated to think of that prognosis for Kiana's friend. "We can't do anything for her now," Dev said. "It's up to the doctors and, more importantly, Tish's body to recover from her injuries. We won't know what that recovery will entail until she wakes up."

"I know. In the meantime, we need to find Meredith." Kiana leaned over Tish and kissed her cheek. "We'll find her," she whispered. When she straightened, she turned to Reid.

"I'll take care of her safety," Reid promised. "Keep me informed on your progress."

"We will," Kiana said. "Let us know of any changes, big or small."

Reid nodded. "Go. Find your friend." To Dev, he said, "Lean on Hawk if you need backup." He handed a key fob to Dev and told him where he'd parked. "Get what you need out of the trunk and bring back my keys."

Dev's fingers curled around the fob. 'Will do." He turned to Kiana. "Ready?"

"I am." With one last glance at Tish lying against the stark white sheets, her brown hair a dark contrast to the bleached white pillowcase, Kiana turned toward the door.

Dev reached for her hand and held it all the way out of the hospital and into the parking lot.

Between Reid's directions and the unlock button

on the fob that blinked headlights and taillights and emitted a short honk, they were able to find the rental car quickly and transfer several cases containing weapons and ammunition to Dev's rental car. Along with the firearms, Dev grabbed a few radio headsets and tossed them in with the guns. The last item he claimed was a wicked black knife in a sheath. He didn't throw it into the truck of the rental car. Instead, he clipped it to his belt.

Kiana gave a short bark of laughter and swallowed hard. "Are we going to war?"

Dev shrugged. "Better to have it and not need it than to need it and not have it." He clipped a knife encased in a sheath onto his belt and grabbed a case containing a small stun gun. When he was finished, he locked both vehicles, grabbed Kiana's hand and headed back into the hospital. "I'd let you sit out in the rental car, but I don't feel comfortable leaving you alone."

"I would've locked the doors," she said.

"Windows can be broken, and glass doesn't stop bullets or baseball bats." His fingers tightened around hers as they stepped into the elevator. "I feel better when you're in my sight."

Kiana punched the button for the floor number for the ICU and gave a gentle squeeze back. "I get it. I feel better knowing Reid's with Tish. I can't imagine leaving her alone in the hospital. She couldn't defend herself when she was conscious. I can't imagine how easy it would be to…" She visibly gulped.

"Reid's there," Dev said softly. "He won't let anything happen to her."

They exited the elevator and hurried to Tish's room. Dev knocked on the door.

Reid opened it a crack, his eyes narrowed. When he saw it was Dev and Kiana, he grinned. "Oh, it's you. Back so soon?"

Dev dropped the key fob in Reid's hand. "Thanks for bringing the supplies."

"No problem." Reid slipped the key fob into his pocket. "Patterson insists on his guys having what they need to do the job."

"And trusts us to use only what's necessary," Dev finished.

"Damn right," Reid said.

They exchanged a wrist clasp in all seriousness.

Kiana glanced past Reid. "Tish?"

Reid shook his head. "Still the same."

She nodded and looked into Dev's eyes. "Ready?"

"We'll be in touch," Dev said and guided Kiana to the elevator.

"I take it you two have worked together in the past," Kiana stated. "I mean, you all arrived on Maui at the same time, but you weren't just a random group of guys showing up at the same time, were you?"

Dev chuckled. "We all served in various branches of the military in spec ops. Special Operations. We left the military for different reasons and signed on with a company that needed, in effect, military security for non-military personnel in foreign countries."

Kiana cocked an eyebrow. "You were mercenaries?"

"Basically." Dev held her door for her as she slipped into the passenger seat of the rental car. He rounded the car to the driver's side.

"What brought you to Hawaii?" she asked, buckling her seatbelt.

"When the US pulled out of Afghanistan, the people we supported had to leave in a hurry. We left as well. There weren't many gigs available to us. Fortunately, Hank Patterson heard we were looking for work and offered to bring our team on board with the newly established Hawaiian office of the Brotherhood Protectors." He started the car and pulled out of the hospital parking lot. "Where to?"

"The escort agency." Kiana keyed an address into the map application on her smartphone and hit GO.

Following the voice instructions from Kiana's phone, Dev maneuvered through the busy streets of Honolulu. "You know my story. What's yours? Especially in connection to your friends, Tish and Meredith."

Kiana stared out the front windshield, her lips

pressed into a tight line. "Tish, Meredith and I were products of the foster care system in Hawaii. At one point, the three of us landed in the same home. Because we had no other family we knew of, we relied on each other for emotional support. Most of our foster families were more interested in the money they were paid to foster children than the children themselves."

"What happened to your parents?" Dev asked.

Kiana shrugged. "Tish is the only one of us who knew her mother and father. They were killed in a boating accident when she was six."

"And yours?" Dev persisted.

Kiana's lips twisted. "I don't have any memories of my father or mother. From state records, my mother abandoned me at a fire station when I was a toddler. They turned me over to social services, and I was placed in foster care."

"Where you met Tish and Meredith," Dev concluded.

"Eventually," Kiana said. "I'm two years older than Meredith and four years older than Tish. I was passed from home to home for a few years with nothing more than what I could stuff into a trash bag. Tish, Meredith and I landed in the same foster home when I was ten. All three of us had long brown hair, were thin and lanky and looked enough alike that we called ourselves sisters. Meredith and I had green eyes. Though Tish's eyes were brown, it didn't matter. She was our little sister, and we loved her. It was the happiest any of us had ever been. We were there for four years until we were shuffled again."

"Why?" Dev asked.

Kiana's lips twisted. "Our foster mom had to give us up when her sister was jailed for check fraud. When her sister, a single parent, went to jail, our foster mom had to take in her sister's four children. Though she hated letting us go, she didn't have room for the three of us. We were split up and sent to three different foster homes."

Though Kiana spoke in a matter-of-fact tone, Dev sensed the underlying sadness she must have experienced being separated from the only family she'd known. "I'm sorry."

Kiana shrugged. "We swore that when we turned eighteen, we'd get an apartment together and look out for each other." She smiled tightly. "Since I was the oldest, I was first to get out. I rented a room over a garage that was barely big enough to call an apartment. It leaked when it rained. I worked two jobs to afford the rent and a scooter to get me back and forth to work."

"How did you break into modeling?" Dev asked.

Kiana smiled. "I landed a job waiting tables at Dukes. The tips were good, and you never knew who would walk in. I was working a table one evening when a talent agent gave me his card. I called and went in for an interview. They were looking for someone tall with dark hair and dark skin who looked Hawaiian. There were other girls there with dark hair and dark skin. Most of them were shorter and had brown eyes. I think they liked that I had green eyes. I was just different enough to get their attention."

Dev smiled. Kiana didn't give herself enough credit. She was stunningly beautiful with her long, lithe body, lush, thick hair and those green eyes that seemed to look straight into your soul. The talent agent had seen her potential. He hadn't been stupid.

"I was hired to model for a local advertising agency, doing a spread on Hawaiian tourism. The work paid well enough for me to get a bigger apartment. When Meredith turned eighteen, she moved in with me. I eventually got her on with the same agent modeling."

Dev shot a glance toward her. "Did you like the work?"

Kiana stared out the side window. "I did. It was the first time in my life I didn't feel like an inconvenience."

Dev maneuvered through traffic without responding. What could he say? Having grown up with both parents who'd loved him unconditionally, he couldn't imagine what it was like to go through childhood without that safety net.

"I learned quickly," Kiana continued. "People liked

that I wasn't a diva, like some of the other models. When Tish came of age, she joined us and got into modeling as well. We did work for catalogs, swimwear, local fashion shows, and hotels. When there were big breaks between modeling jobs, we hired on with Aloha Escorts, making it very clear to their management that we weren't prostitutes, and sex wasn't part of the job. We preferred to meet our clients at public places, getting our own transportation to and from."

"That was smart," Dev said. "Was it enough?"

"For the most part. We carried little cans of mace in our purses."

"Did you ever use it?"

Her lips curled for a moment. "Once, when a man didn't understand the concept of *No*." Kiana lifted her chin. "I'd always wondered if that little can of mace really worked." She shot a glance toward Dev. "It did."

"Do you still carry it?"

She nodded. "Like you so wisely stated earlier, it's better to have it and not need it than need it and not have it."

"Good to know." He grinned. "Remind me not to make you mad."

The directions led Dev past a shopping mall, a row of businesses and a convenience store, where he turned and drove through a mix of apartment buildings and smaller businesses. As he neared their destination, Kiana leaned forward.

"It's the building just past the dive shop," she said. "Go past it, turn left and park behind the building."

He did as she directed and parked at the back of a building that appeared to be a business on the ground floor with apartments above. A small brass sign hung over the back door with the words ALOHA ESCORTS written in fading black letters. The building had been painted a dark gray at some point. Sun and salty air had taken its toll on the paint, making it curl and flake.

Kiana stared through the windshield. "It looks even seedier than when I was here last." She shrugged. "It's not like the escorts hang around inside. There are usually only a few people here: Cliff, the manager; Niko, the runner; and Rose, the secretary. Cliff and Rose field the calls, schedule the escorts and run payroll. Niko does whatever errands Cliff and Rose have for him. If an escort's car isn't working, Niko will get that person where she needs to be on time. If a girl gets in a jam, he bails her out."

"Does he do that often?" Dev unbuckled his seatbelt.

"More often than you'd think. Mostly because the client has passed out drunk or has left without the escort."

Dev slid out of the driver's seat and hurried around to open Kiana's door. He held out his hand and helped her to her feet.

She hesitated, staring at the building.

"What?"

Kiana shook her head. "When I left Oahu, I swore I was done with this life. It feels surreal being back here."

"Are you afraid?" he asked.

"Of these people?" Kiana shook her head. "Of stepping back into this life? Yeah. I guess so." She gave him a shaky smile. "I don't like living paycheck to paycheck, wondering when I'll get the next call for a modeling job. I hated having to supplement my income as an escort. Sure, modeling was fun and exciting at first. But it was like being a foster kid. You never knew how long it would last. One day, everything would be great. The next, you were worried about being thrown out because you couldn't pay the rent, or your foster family didn't want you living there anymore."

Dev touched a hand to the small of her back. "You've got a job on Maui as the manager of a major resort. A steady job, as far as I could tell. You don't have to come back to Oahu to live."

She shook her head. "The problem is, I feel responsible for Meredith and Tish. I never should've left them. We were supposed to look out for each other. It's my fault Meredith is missing, and Tish was attacked. I failed them by leaving."

"You didn't attack Tish, and you didn't make Meredith disappear," he reminded her.

"If I had stayed," Kiana said, "none of this would've happened."

Dev pulled her up against him and brushed his lips across the top of her head. "You don't know that. Beating yourself up over something you couldn't control is a waste of energy."

"You're right." Kiana squared her shoulders. "I need to focus on what I *can* do, not what I *should* have done. Let's find Cliff and hear what he has to say about Meredith's client."

Dev wanted to say more, to reassure Kiana that she wasn't to blame for what had happened to her sisters of the heart. Bad shit happened whether you were there or not. He knew it, had experienced it and could do nothing to change the course of events after the fact.

Dev and Kiana climbed the steps.

Before Dev could raise his hand to knock, Kiana reached for the doorknob, turned it and pushed the door open.

Dev raised his arm in front of her to keep her from stepping inside. He pointed to the concrete porch and whispered, "Stay."

"But—" she started.

He shook his head and repeated, "Stay." Though his tone was hushed, she responded to the command by planting her feet firmly on the concrete with every intention of staying right where he'd pointed.

Dev rested his hand on the hilt of the knife

clipped to his belt and eased through the open door into a shadowy interior.

He hadn't gone two steps when cold metal pressed against his temple.

A deep voice sounded from behind him. "My finger's shaking. If you move even an inch, I can't be responsible for blowing off your head."

CHAPTER 4

STANDING on the porch outside the Aloha Escorts office, Kiana bristled at being told to stay when she was the one who knew this office and the people who ran it.

When Dev froze just inside the doorway, Kiana left the spot he'd pointed to and stepped up behind him. "Look, I know these people," she said, "you don't. Let me—" Kiana came to an abrupt halt, the air leaving her lungs at the sight of the cool gray metal of a gun barrel pressed to Dev's temple. "What the h—"

"Kiana," Dev said softly. "Get back."

Before she could follow his order, the door swung wider.

Daylight shone in on the blond-haired man holding the gun to Dev's head. The man wore his signature light gray pin-stripe suit, but his hair wasn't neatly slicked back with a ton of product like Kiana remembered. It stuck out at odd angles.

Kiana opened her mouth to say something.

Before she could get a word out, Dev moved in a blur of motion, snatched the gun from Cliff and turned it around to point at the older man.

Cliff held up his hands in surrender. "Call him off, Kiana. I didn't know he was with you."

Kiana reached out and placed her hand on Dev's arm. "It's okay. This is Cliff Rey, the man we came to talk with. Cliff, meet Devlin Mulhaney. He's new on Oahu and looking for work."

"Can't help you." Cliff backed away from Dev, rubbing the wrist Dev had knocked aside while stealing the pistol. "The office is closed until further notice."

Kiana blinked. "Closed? Why?" Her eyes narrowed as she studied his face.

The closer Kiana looked, the more she could see of Cliff's face. One eye was swollen, a dark purple bruise spread across his cheek and his lip was split, with dried blood in the corner. "What the hell happened?"

Cliff raised a hand to touch his lip. He winced and shook his head. "I'm not sure. I'd just sent Rose out to get us a late lunch. Niko was out delivering four of our escorts to a convention. I had the place to myself when a couple of guys walked into the building wearing ski masks."

Kiana gasped. "Did they rob you?"

He snorted. "I wish. No, they wanted information."

"What information?" Dev asked.

"They wanted to know where Kiana's friend, Meredith, was."

Kiana's heart squeezed tightly in her chest. She touched Cliff's arm. "Do you know where she is?"

Cliff laughed and clutched his side. "Do you think that if I'd known where she was, I would look like this?" He pointed to his face. "I'd have told them and spared my face and ribs." He shook his head. "If not for my upstairs neighbor shouting, *I'm calling the cops*, those guys might've finished me off."

"Sweet Jesus," Kiana murmured. "Did the cops come?"

Cliff nodded. "They left a few minutes before you got here. I called Rose and told her to go home and lock the door. I told Niko to stay away from the office until further notice."

"What about you?" Kiana asked. "The cops didn't call for an ambulance? Should you still be here instead of a hospital?"

Cliff shot a glance past Kiana and Dev, out into the street as if looking for his attackers. Apparently satisfied for the moment that they weren't lurking nearby, Cliff motioned Kiana and Dev across the threshold and closed the door behind them. When he switched on the light, Dev whistled.

"Wow," Kiana stared at the mess. Chairs had been turned over, a file cabinet's drawers lay on the floor, the documents inside covering the worn carpet. "They did this?"

"In between using me as a punching bag." Cliff shoved a hand through his hair. "When I wouldn't tell them anything they wanted to hear about Meredith, they turned my office upside down, digging through my files. I'm glad they did. It was the noise that pissed off my neighbor who works night shift."

"Did they find what they were looking for?" Dev asked.

Cliff shook his head. "The file cabinets are only for paper copies of bills paid and insurance policies. We don't keep any paper documents about escorts or clients. That information is encrypted in our online files." He bent to lift a fallen office chair but moaned and stopped short.

"Let me." Dev set the chair back onto its wheels.

"Thanks." Cliff rolled the chair to a desk in the corner where a monitor lay face-down on the keyboard. He stood the monitor up and checked the power cord. "I hope they didn't destroy my computer." He laughed and groaned, holding onto his side.

Cliff tipped his head toward a door standing open to an empty cabinet at the base of the desk. "They took the old CPU. Not that they'll get anything out of it. I cleared the files when we upgraded to this expensive model with the CPU enclosed in the monitor."

Cliff touched a button on the keyboard. Moments later, the monitor lit up with a login screen.

The Aloha Escorts manager let go of a relieved breath. "Thank God. It's still working. I passed on the ambulance because I wanted to look through our files for information on Meredith." He frowned. "If you've seen her, you might want to warn her that someone came looking for her here."

"I stopped by her apartment," Kiana said. "Her roommate said she hadn't heard from her since she'd said she was doing an escort job a week ago."

"Tish?" Cliff didn't look up from the monitor. "I haven't heard from her in weeks. Modeling gigs must be good. How is she?"

"I just left her at the hospital in a coma," Kiana stated, her tone flat. "Someone broke into her apartment and beat the shit out of her."

Cliff swore. "I'm sorry to hear that. Do you think it has anything to do with the people who came here looking for Meredith?"

"I don't know," Kiana said, though she suspected it did. She stepped closer. "You keep all the client and escort information on this CPU?"

"Yup," Cliff said. "And everything is backed up to encrypted files in the cloud." He poked at the keyboard, flipping through screens one at a time. "Rose is so much faster at this. I never heard back from Meredith or the client after her last assignment. Since we collect payment upfront, I didn't think to check in with her. I assumed all went well. Then we got slammed by a local convention…" He punched a button and sighed. "I should've checked on her. I usually do if an escort doesn't report in after a job. You know that's one of the rules we stress."

"I remember." Yeah, he should have checked on her. Kiana bit down hard on her tongue to keep from telling him just that.

Cliff continued to peck at the keyboard with two fingers, moving so slowly that Kiana wanted to take over or scream or send the guys on a mission to hijack this man's communications devices.

Cliff glanced over his shoulder. "Why are you back? I thought you'd moved to Maui?"

"I did," Kiana said. "But I found Dev. He needs work and couldn't find anything on Maui, so I brought him here to see if you could use him as an escort."

"I don't know. It might be a while before I feel comfortable sending anyone else out, male or female." Cliff's gaze quickly ran over Dev from head to toe before he looked back at the monitor. "But he might work for the ladies who call us. Check back in a few days after my pulse returns to normal and I don't jump at every noise."

Kiana could understand that. After encountering Tish's attacker, she was jumpy and constantly looking over her shoulder.

"Oh, there," he pointed at the monitor, "Meredith

was scheduled to meet with a man who signed up as Tony Baretta." Cliff's lips curled in a sneer. "Like so many clients, he didn't want to give his real name. These guys usually give us a business credit card number and expense their escort as entertainment. We require a photo of our clients so our escorts can identify them when they make contact." Cliff clicked another key, and an image of a man appeared on the monitor. He had dark, thinning hair and a plain, nice face with light gray or blue eyes.

As far as Kiana could tell, the man didn't look like a murderer.

But then, no one had suspected Ted Bundy of being a murderer and serial killer. He'd appeared to be a fine, upstanding citizen to most people, even to the women he'd killed...at first.

"Can we get that photo and the credit card number?" Dev asked. "I know someone who might be able to figure out his real name."

Cliff frowned at Dev and then at Kiana. "Is he kidding me?"

Kiana shook her head. "If you can't tell us who the client was, I need anything you have on him. Meredith might be in trouble. I need to find her."

"You know I don't share that kind of information," Cliff said. "Not even with the police without a search warrant."

"Meredith is my friend," Kiana said. "You should

have checked on her. Hell, you should be looking this guy up. What if he's hurt her?"

"We don't know that he's the reason she disappeared," Cliff argued.

"And we won't until we have a chance to talk to him." Kiana touched the manager's shoulder. "It's Meredith we're talking about. Those men who tried to kill you today were looking for her. Wouldn't you rather we found her than them?"

Cliff's brow knitted. "I want her found, so they'll quit coming after me." He rested a hand on his ribs and winced. "Fine. I'll give you whatever I have as long as you don't do anything stupid with it, like blackmail him."

"I promise." Kiana held up her hand as if swearing in a court. "My only concern is Meredith. Once I find her, I'll shred the guy's number."

On a notepad, Cliff jotted down the name the client had given, his cell phone number and the number from the credit card he'd used to pay for the escort encounter. Once Cliff had the information recorded, he tore the sheet off the pad and handed it to Kiana. "Let me know what you find…as soon as you find it."

"Yes, sir." Kiana tucked the sheet of paper into her pocket and reached for Dev's hand.

"Ready?" he asked, curling his fingers around hers.

"I am," Kiana answered softly. "Thank you, Cliff."

"I'm sure we won't be shut down for long," Cliff said. "Come back and see me in a few days if you want work. Both of you."

Dev stepped out of the building before Kiana and looked around for a moment. Then, he pulled her into the curve of his arm and hustled her out to the rental car. Once she was safely in the passenger seat, he rounded the front and slid behind the wheel. "Can I see the information Cliff gave you?"

Kiana dug the folded paper out of her pocket and handed it to Dev.

He pulled out his cell phone and snapped a photo of the writing.

"What are you going to do with the information?" Kiana asked.

"I'm sending it to Hank Patterson, the leader of the Brotherhood Protectors. He has a computer guru named Swede who can find anything about anyone using a computer."

Kiana frowned. "If the client didn't use his real name, will Swede be able to find him?"

"Absolutely," Dev said with a grin. "From what Hank Patterson told us, he's good. Really good."

"I hope he does it quickly." Kiana stared through the front windshield. "Time isn't standing still for Meredith. We need to get to her before the other people who are looking for her and before whoever might be holding her hostage harms her."

"I texted Swede with a reminder that we needed

the information ASAP." He pocketed his cell phone and gripped the gear shift. "Where to now?"

"Hold on for a minute." Kiana dug her cell phone out of her purse. "Let me call her agent and see if he's heard from her."

"Agent?"

"Modeling." Kiana scrolled through her contacts and selected the number for the agent she, Meredith and Tish had used to secure modeling gigs. The phone rang four times. Kiana prepared to leave a message when a male voice answered.

"Arquette Talent Agency, Troy Arquette speaking."

"Troy, it's Kiana Williams."

"Kiana, sweetheart," he said in the effusive style Kiana remembered so well. "Please tell me you're back on Oahu and ready to work."

"I am back in Oahu, but I'm not looking for work."

"No? I'm sorry to hear that. I have a job that would fit you perfectly."

"I'm not modeling anymore, Troy," Kiana said.

"That's a shame," Troy said. "I tried to get in touch with your friend Meredith, but she's not responding to my calls or texts. I don't suppose you know how I can connect with her, do you? I needed someone… well…yesterday."

"When was the last time you spoke with Meredith?" Kiana asked.

"I don't know," Troy answered. "I suppose a little over a week ago. She called to see if I had any work for her. I'd just signed Tish for a shoot on Kauai, but I didn't have anything at the time for Meredith. The job I have for her now came up two days ago. She usually responds to my calls within twenty-four hours."

"Has anyone come by your office asking about Meredith?" Kiana asked.

"No," Troy said. "Why do you ask? Has something happened to Meredith?"

Kiana sighed. "She's been missing for almost a week."

"Seriously?" Troy muttered a curse. "Did you check with the escort agency she used when she needed extra cash?"

Kiana stared at the Aloha Escorts office. "I just left the escort office. They haven't seen her since her last assignment."

"Damn," Troy said. "I told her working as an escort was dangerous."

"Yeah, well, we're not the only ones looking for her. You might want to lock your doors. Tish is in the hospital after someone broke into her and Meredith's apartment. A couple of big guys just roughed up the manager at the escort service, looking for Meredith."

Tony whistled. "No shit?"

"Yeah. Consider this a heads-up. Whoever's looking for Meredith is playing rough. They might pay you a visit next." Kiana glanced at Dev. "Be careful."

"Locking my doors now," Tony said. "And, Kiana, you be careful as well. And, just so you know, I haven't given up hope that you'll come back to work with me."

"I like working in the resort industry. It's a lot steadier than modeling, and I won't age out of it too soon," she said. "But I'll keep you in mind."

Kiana ended the call and gave Dev a twisted smile. "I guess you heard most of that."

He nodded. "Her agent hasn't heard from her either." His eyes narrowed. "Do you trust him? For that matter, do you trust your friend Cliff?" He tilted his head toward the building in front of him.

Kiana shrugged. "I've never had reason not to. He did his best to give us clients who wouldn't take advantage of us. Besides, he has other escorts who will do anything for a price."

Dev's eyes narrowed more. "The escort business can be shady, at best."

Kiana sighed. "Yeah, but it helped pay the rent when the modeling jobs didn't come through. I'd have gone back to being a waitress, but I had to be flexible enough to take a modeling job whenever one came up. The better places to be a waitress weren't as flexible with their schedules, and rightfully so. They handle a huge number of customers. Tourist season is all year long in Hawaii. Especially in Waikiki."

Dev reached out and touched her arm. "I'm not judging."

"Thanks," she said. "And you're right. The escort business has its shady side."

He returned his hand to the steering wheel. "Is there anywhere else we should look for Meredith? Anyone she might have contacted or gone to if she was in trouble?"

"Maybe her boyfriend. Hopefully, whoever trashed Cliff's office hasn't found him yet." Kiana bit her bottom lip. "The problem is, I don't know where he lives."

"You know his name?" Dev asked.

"Jason Ungers." Her brow furrowed. "Meredith started seeing him after I moved to Maui. In our phone conversations, she never said where he lived, just that he worked as a bartender on the evening shift at a place called The Big Wave Dive Bar." She glanced at her watch. "It's a little early for the bar to be open. Could we check in with Reid and see if there's any change in Tish's condition?"

Dev nodded. "We should grab something to eat. I can call Reid and also check in with Swede to see if he's found anything on the internet."

Kiana's stomach rumbled loudly at his mention of food. She was shocked that the day had flown by, and it wouldn't be long before the sun set on the island. "You must be starving."

"I could eat," he admitted. "And so should you."

She rested her hand over her belly. "I feel oddly guilty thinking of eating when my friends are in such dire straits."

"You're no help to them if you don't keep up your strength," he said. "Food fuels your body and your mind."

She sighed. "I know. It's just that we're no closer to finding Meredith or the people who hurt Tish and Cliff." Kiana wrung her hands in her lap. "What has Meredith gotten herself into?"

"I don't know." Dev shifted into drive. "But I'm worried about you."

Kiana's eyebrows rose. "Why me?"

Dev's jaw tightened. "I think some really bad assholes would kill to find her. Now that you're in town, you might be their next target."

CHAPTER 5

KIANA GAVE Dev directions to a restaurant close to The Big Wave Dive Bar.

Dev navigated Honolulu traffic, one light at a time until they neared the bar and restaurant.

"They won't have anywhere to park at either establishment." She pointed to a place past the restaurant on the right. "There's a parking lot a block ahead on the left."

He pulled into a paid parking lot and backed into a parking space. Using an online app, he paid for the parking for the space number and locked the car.

Together, they walked to a small grill where they ordered hamburgers and fries. Dev had tea while Kiana drank water with a slice of lemon.

Kiana picked at her food, eating a quarter of her burger and leaving most of her fries untouched.

After Dev had consumed his last fry, he called Swede.

"Hey, Dev," Hank's computer guy answered on the first ring. "Glad you called."

Dev hit the speaker button and turned the volume down so that only he and Kiana could hear the conversation at their table. "You're on speaker in a restaurant with Kiana and me. Did you find anything?"

"As a matter of fact, I did," Swede said. "And it's not good news."

Dev glanced across at Kiana.

She gave a quick nod.

"Shoot," Dev said.

"First off," Swede began, "the name you gave me did not match the name linked to the credit card."

Dev held Kiana's gaze. "We didn't think it would. Who is the guy who booked Meredith through the escort service?"

"Hugh Thompson," Swede said. "He owns a chain of dry-cleaning businesses on the California coast. Apparently, he was in Honolulu for a weekend conference of dry cleaners."

"Anything hinky in his background?" Dev asked.

"No. Just a married man with a wife and two teenage children going to a private school in Los Angeles," Swede said.

"Think he was capable of kidnapping Meredith O'Neil?" Dev asked.

"I don't think he's capable of kidnapping anyone," Swede said.

"No," Dev frowned. "Why?"

"Because I ran a scan through the Honolulu police database for the past week and found his name listed."

"An arrest?" Kiana asked.

"No, ma'am," Swede responded. "A homicide."

Kiana gasped. "Committed or victim?"

Swede hesitated for a second, then answered, "Victim."

Kiana's face paled.

"A hotel worker found him the morning after his scheduled date with Ms. O'Neil."

Dev reached across the table for her hand. "Did you dive deep enough for the full report?"

"I did," Swede said. "He was found in his rental car behind a hotel, a bullet hole through the front wind-shield and his forehead."

Kiana slumped over the table, her hand squeezing Dev's.

"Any sign of a woman in the vehicle with him?" Dev asked.

Kiana squeezed his hand harder, her body shaking.

"The victim was the only one in the vehicle."

Dev hated asking, but he had to know. "Any other blood in the vehicle belonging to anyone but the dead Mr. Thompson?"

"No," Swede responded. "They dusted the car for prints. Nothing definitive has been reported about his killer. No matches yet on any fingerprints other than the victim's."

"Whoever shot him through the windshield wouldn't have left fingerprints," Dev said. "And, unless Ms. O'Neil has been arrested at some point in her life, her prints won't show up on any database."

Kiana frowned. "If she was taken from the vehicle, whoever took her might have left their prints on the door handle."

"In which case," Swede continued, "they might not have had fingerprints stored in the databases."

Dev tapped a finger on the table. "Or they wore gloves."

"That's assuming Ms. O'Neil was taken from the vehicle," Swede said. "What if she got out on her own?"

Kiana shook her head from side to side. "Or maybe she never was in the vehicle. If she continued treating the escort service as we promised each other we would, she never would've gotten into the car with the stranger. She'd have met him either in the lobby of the event or out front, in a well-lit area."

Dev shook his head. "Any security camera footage from nearby businesses?"

"There was only one camera at the back of the hotel," Swede said.

Dev held his breath, waiting for Swede to fill him in on what he'd found.

"Non-operational," Swede stated. "The folks performing the investigation have yet to find a match on the fingerprints database."

Kiana shook her head, glancing around the dining room as if looking for answers and finding none. "Why kill the client? If someone wanted Meredith, why bother killing the man?"

Dev's eyes narrowed. "Perhaps the killer showed up at the event in his place, claiming to be Hugh Thompson."

"Sweet Jesus," Kiana whispered. "She wouldn't have known it wasn't him. If the guy who took his place showed up at the event, claiming he was Hugh, Meredith would only have had a photo provided by the service. Those photos aren't always the best quality. If the guy who showed up looked even slightly like the photo, claiming he was Hugh, she probably would've accepted it as true."

"If she went with the imposter Hugh, who is still looking for her?" Dev asked.

"Which leads me to believe she might have figured out he wasn't her client, and she got away before he could kidnap her." Swede tipped his head to the side. "But why not go directly to the police and let them know she was kidnapped or being stalked?"

Kiana sat back in her seat. "At this point, we don't know anything other than the man she was supposed to meet is dead. We don't know if Meredith was taken or if she left on her own." She sighed. "We need more information."

Dev glanced at his watch. "The bar should be opening in the next ten minutes. Let's find Meredith's boyfriend. Maybe he has a clue as to her whereabouts."

"I'll keep searching the internet for any data about the client and the escort service," Swede said.

"What about the modeling agency?" Dev asked.

"I looked, but there's not a lot on the agency or her agent," he said. "I'll keep digging."

As soon as Dev ended the call, his cell phone chirped.

He glanced at the screen, and a smile curled the corners of his lips. He answered, "Hey, asshole. Let me guess, you're bored and want in on the action."

George Ingram chuckled. "I have to admit, I'm ready for my first assignment as a Brotherhood Protector. What's this I hear about you being on Oahu with your first assignment? Why didn't they give it to one of the guys already here?"

"Because you're a bunch of dirtbags, and only the best could handle this." Dev winked across at a frowning Kiana. "Seriously, my client was on Maui when I got the assignment."

Again, George chuckled. "I know. Hawk gave us the heads-up to be ready in case you needed backup."

"Thanks." Dev's chest swelled. He knew he could

count on his team for support. The guys he'd come to Hawaii with had worked together and knew each other. Dev had served with some of them on active duty. He'd come to know the others while working as contracted security in Afghanistan. Mercenaries, as Kiana had called them. They'd all come from special operations backgrounds. They knew the importance of trusting your team to have your six.

It was also nice knowing Hawk was a step ahead, alerting the team members who'd landed on Oahu for their island familiarization time.

Dev could count on George, a former Marine Force Recon. He was a complete badass who'd charge into an enemy-held position without fear, shooting from both hips. Rex Johnson and Logan Atkins, both former Delta Force, were no less impressive. They'd come to the party in a heartbeat if he got into a tight place, which could happen based on the attacks on Hugh, Tish and Cliff.

"Let us know if we can be of any assistance in your search for the missing woman," George said.

"I will. We're heading to the bar where Ms. O'Neil's ex-boyfriend works."

"Oh yeah?" George said. "Which one?"

"The Big Wave," Dev said.

"Ha." George laughed. "We've been there. It's a little off the beaten path. Attracts more locals."

"Good to know. Headed there now."

"Let us know if we can help," George reminded him.

"Will do." Dev ended the call.

"Someone you know is on Oahu?" Kiana asked.

Dev nodded. "We came to Hawaii as a team to work for the Brotherhood Protectors. Our regional boss, Hawk, thought it would be a good idea for us to familiarize ourselves with the lay of the land and split us up on a few of the islands. Reid, Angel, Teller and I landed on Maui. George, Rex and Logan got Oahu, and the others are on Kauai."

Kiana's eyes widened. "I hadn't realized until now that there were more than the four of you I met on Maui and your boss, Hawk."

"Hank Patterson thought it would be a good idea to have an office here, considering how many people visit and how far it is from the mainland."

"I'm glad he made that decision," Kiana said softly. "I'd hate to think of looking for Meredith on my own. And it comforts me to know your friend Reid is looking out for Tish while she's defenseless in the hospital." She drew in a deep breath. "I'm so worried for Meredith. I can't imagine what trouble she's in. I hope she's okay."

Dev reached across the table for Kiana's hand. "We'll find her."

She laid her hand in his. "Thank you for helping."

He squeezed her fingers gently. "Ready?"

Kiana nodded.

Dev waved down the waitress, paid the bill and escorted Kiana out of the restaurant.

As they walked the short distance to the bar, Dev remained fully aware of their surroundings. While they'd been at the restaurant, the sun had set, streetlights glowed and people hurried along the streets in cars, on bicycles and walking, in a hurry to get home or to work in the service industry.

At the entrance to The Big Wave, Dev held the door for Kiana. As she passed through, he took her hand and held it all the way to the bar. He wanted the other patrons to think they were together to eliminate the added distraction of other men hitting on the beautiful Kiana. If he were them, he'd want to.

Her native Hawaiian beauty had captivated him the first time he'd seen her at the resort on Maui. From the moment they'd checked in, she'd made it abundantly clear she wasn't interested in anything more than a business relationship. When he'd volunteered to take the mission, she'd spelled it out. He remembered what she'd said, word for word.

"I don't need a date. I don't want a relationship. I'm not going to fall in love with you. I'd appreciate it if you'd refrain from hitting on me, calling me sweetheart, and, for God's sake, don't fancy yourself falling in love with me."

He'd liked her frankness and spunk. He also liked how her hand felt in his—strong yet supple, her skin soft against his. At that moment, he imagined those hands sliding across his naked body.

Dev's groin tightened.

Hell, he needed to shut down those thoughts immediately. Falling in love with her was out of the question. That didn't stop his body from responding to her nearness.

He wondered why she was so adamant about not wanting a relationship. There had to be a reason. Some bastard might have broken her heart.

Dev found two bar stools at the far end of the bar and helped Kiana up into hers before settling in beside her.

The bartender, an older, burly man with short, spiked gray hair, was busy filling beer mugs from the tap. Once he set them on a tray for the waitress, he made his way to the end of the bar where Dev and Kiana sat. "What can I get you?"

Kiana gave the bartender her lovely smile. "White wine."

The bartender nodded and looked at Dev.

"Whiskey on the rocks," Dev said.

When the bartender turned away to fill their orders, Kiana leaned close to Dev. "That's not Jason."

"Do you know what he looks like?" Dev asked.

"Meredith sent me a picture of the two of them a while back. Let me find it." Kiana pulled her cell phone from her purse and scrolled through text messages from Meredith.

The bartender returned with their drinks at the

same time Kiana found the photo she was looking for.

"There," she said, sliding her phone across the bar toward Dev. "That's Meredith and Jason."

The bartender stared at the image and frowned. "You know Jason?"

Kiana smiled up at the man behind the bar. "No, but I know his girlfriend."

The bartender nodded. "I've seen her around."

"Jason works here, right?" Kiana asked.

"He did," the bartender said.

"Can I get another beer?" a customer at the other end of the bar called out.

The bartender hurried to fill the man's order and several for a waitress who'd come to the bar with a load of empty bottles, glasses and mugs.

"What did he mean Jason did work here?" Kiana chewed on her bottom lip.

"We'll ask when the man gets another break between customers," Dev assured her. He sipped the whiskey with no intention of finishing the drink. He wanted to keep a clear head. Alcohol dulled his senses. Dev had a gut feeling he'd need his wits about him.

The bartender worked his way back down the bar, filling mugs and mixing drinks. When he finally made it back to Dev and Kiana, he asked, "Ready for another?"

Kiana shook her head. "What did you mean when you said Jason did work here? Did he quit?"

The man snorted. "He might as well have quit. He's been a no-show for the past week. The boy never checked in to say he was sick or wouldn't make his shift. I had to work a double three times this week. I tried to call him. No answer. I went by his place and knocked. No answer. If you see him, tell him not to bother coming back. I got a business to run. I don't like being ghosted by my employees." With that, the bartender turned and walked away.

Kiana reached for Dev's hand. "So, Jason's missing as well."

"Do you think he would have kidnapped Meredith?" Dev asked.

Kiana shrugged. "Why would he? It's not like she's the daughter of a rich man he could hold for ransom. We grew up in the foster system. You'd think if she was his daughter, that the rich man would've found her sooner."

"Unless he didn't know about her until recently," Dev suggested. "You say you didn't know your parents, that you were abandoned as a toddler. What about Meredith?"

Kiana's brow furrowed. "The foster care people told her that she was left at a fire station as an infant. They put her into foster care immediately. Her foster family had her for four years and were getting ready to adopt her when their marriage fell apart, and she was shuffled off to a series of foster homes until she landed at the same home with Tish and me."

Dev's lips twisted. "For all you know, she could've been the bastard child of a celebrity who had an affair with his housekeeper or nanny."

"Right? Neither one of them would've had a birth certificate. It bugged her more than it did me. I figured a mother who would abandon her own child didn't deserve that child. I didn't want to know my mother. She didn't deserve me." Her frown deepened. "Meredith always wanted to know who her birth parents were. She figured her mother was desperate, didn't have a job, couldn't feed a baby and did the only thing she could to save her child."

"She gave her up rather than see her starve or suffer," Dev said. "That could've been your mother as well."

"Maybe," Kiana said. "Meredith wanted to know so badly that I got her a DNA test for her birthday and a subscription to one of those ancestry sites. She made me take one of those DNA tests as well. It told me what I already knew. I'm mostly Hawaiian with a small percentage of Irish and German."

"And Meredith?" Dev asked.

"Same." Kiana's lips twisted. "Mostly Hawaiian with a smattering of Welsh and Mediterranean. I think it was the small percentages that gave us both green eyes."

"Did she find any connections on the ancestry site?"

Kiana tipped her head. "She was just getting into that site a couple of weeks ago." Her lips curled upward. "She was so excited, thinking she might find people she was related to."

"And did she?"

"I don't know. She didn't say." She stared into Dev's eyes. "It might be worth looking into. I bet she had all that stuff on her laptop."

At that moment, Kiana's cell phone buzzed where it lay on the bar.

Kiana frowned at the number. "I don't know anyone at that number." Still, she answered the phone and held it to her ear. "What?" Her face paled, and she looked around the room. "We have to get out of here? Who is this?" She pulled the phone away from her ear and stared at it. "Someone just called and said to get out of the bar. Now."

"Did you recognize the voice?" he asked.

"No. But whoever it was seemed convinced we needed to get out."

Movement out of the corner of Dev's eye caught his attention. Three large men wearing black T-shirts and jeans entered the bar. Each one had similar tattoos from their wrists all the way up their arms and around their necks, like gang members.

When one man waved toward the bar, Dev recognized the tattoo on the inside of his arm as the same stylized tribal mask he'd seen on the man who'd attacked Tish.

These guys had to be from the same gang.

Dev stiffened and slid off his stool. "Your caller might've had the right idea." He gripped Kiana's elbow and helped her down from her stool.

When Kiana started for the door, he steered her away and toward the hallway at the rear, where there was a sign indicating the bathrooms.

"This isn't the way out," Kiana whispered.

"Those three men who just walked in are headed our way. I don't think they'll let us just walk by." He hurried her down the hallway toward the restrooms. There was no rear exit they could duck out. With little time to spare, Dev guided Kiana into the women's bathroom, praying there was a window they could crawl through to get out of the building.

The ladies' bathroom was a dead end with two stalls, two sinks and no windows.

"What do we do now?" Kiana asked.

"We go out the front entrance and pray those men aren't here to stop us." He turned her toward him. "I'll distract them as best I can. You run past them and go to the car." He dug the keys out of his pocket and handed them to her. "If I'm not right behind you, get into the car and drive to the nearest police station."

She shook her head. "I'm not leaving you to handle three men by yourself."

"I need you to get out and away."

When she opened her mouth to protest, he pressed his lips to hers, stemming the flow of words.

It was a brief, hard kiss, but it made her stop talking.

When his head came up, he stared down into her green eyes. "Please. Do as I say. I can handle them."

She nodded, her eyes wide.

"Okay." He set her at arm's length. "I'll go out first and distract them. You come out a few seconds later and head straight for the front door."

He let go of her arms and eased open the door. The hallway was clear. Dev wondered if he was reading something more into the three men showing up when they had.

After a quick glance back at Kiana, Dev walked back to the barroom. The three men stood near the end of the bar closest to the hallway.

When Dev appeared, the lead guy's eyes narrowed. He glanced past Dev as if looking for Kiana.

Not wanting to wait for the men to come to him, Dev advanced on them, smiling. "I've been thinking about getting another tattoo. Where do you suggest I go?"

"Go the fuck to hell," the biggest meanest-looking man said. He planted his hands on Dev's chest and shoved him.

"Shouldn't have done that, man," Dev said. "Now, it's game on."

CHAPTER 6

THE ODDS SUCKED, but Dev had to buy Kiana enough time to get past the three tattooed gang members.

When the biggest guy started to go around him, Dev stuck out his foot and jammed his shoulder into the man at the same time. The man tripped and fell like a ton of bricks, sprawling across the floor on his hands and knees.

When the other two men came at Dev, he bent low and plowed into the first guy like a linebacker. That man fell backward, knocking into the man behind him. They both fell to the floor in a tangle of arms and legs.

Kiana darted out of the hallway and ran.

She'd only gone three steps when the big guy on the floor snagged her ankle.

She staggered and fell to her knees.

Dev spun and kicked the guy hard in the kidney and then stomped on the arm holding Kiana's ankle.

The man loosened his hold enough that Kiana rolled away and scrambled to her feet.

By that time, the two men who'd fallen in a heap on the floor were on their feet.

One man jumped onto Dev's back.

Kiana was halfway across the barroom floor when she glanced over her shoulder.

"Run!" Dev yelled.

Instead, she stopped, turned and grabbed an empty chair.

"No, no, no," Dev muttered. "Run, Kiana!"

The man on his back hooked his arm around him and punched Dev in the face.

Dev grabbed the man's elbow, bent at the waist and flipped him over his head. The man landed on the big guy trying to climb to his feet.

"Dev, duck!" Kiana yelled as she rushed toward him.

He ducked and rolled automatically as she swung the chair toward the position where he'd been standing.

The chair caught the other man who'd come up behind him. It hit him square in the chest but not hard enough to take him down.

Instead, he caught the chair, flung it to the side and rushed toward Kiana.

Dev jumped on the man's back and wrapped an arm around his neck in a chokehold.

The two men on the floor leaped to their feet. Both men ran toward Kiana.

"For God's sake, Kiana, run!" Dev yelled.

The stubborn woman grabbed another chair and pointed the legs at the two men like it would do anything to stop them.

The big man Dev had kicked in the kidney batted the chair from Kiana's hands.

Kiana stepped backward until her back ran into a tall man dressed in a Hawaiian shirt, shorts and dark sunglasses.

The man pulled Kiana behind him into the arms of another man dressed in a white polo shirt and khaki slacks.

The man in the Hawaiian shirt stood in front of the two tattooed men with his arms crossed. "Hey, Dev, it appears you have your hands full. Do you want us to take out the trash?"

George Ingram took off the dark sunglasses, folded them and tucked them into his shirt pocket.

Dev would've sighed with relief if he hadn't been gritting his teeth. He tightened his arm around the throat of the man whose back he was still riding. "If you don't have anything...better to...do."

The man beneath him bucked and clawed at the arm around his throat.

"You can only drink so many Mai Tais before—" George started.

The big man lunged toward George.

For a tall man, George was quick on his feet. He stepped to the side and grabbed the tattooed man's arm, twisted it behind his back and shoved him face-first to the floor.

When the other man rushed George, Rex Johnson pushed Kiana behind him.

Rex turned back in time to intercept the second man with a hard jab to the gut. As the man doubled over, Rex caught him on the chin with a wicked uppercut. Before the man could regain his balance, Rex planted a well-placed sidekick to his chest, sending him flying backward into a table.

The table broke beneath the man's weight and crashed to the floor.

"I called the police," the bartender yelled. "They're on their way."

The man Dev was holding onto finally fell to his knees.

Dev released his hold around the guy's neck and shoved him forward.

He landed on his hands, sucking air into his lungs.

George and Rex stood with their fists clenched in a ready stance.

"Dev, get your girl and get out," George said. "We'll hold them long enough to give you a head start."

Dev moved toward Kiana, frowning. "That'll leave you three to two."

"We'll be fine," George assured him.

"We've had worse odds," Rex said. "Besides, Logan's on his way. He should be here soon."

"Go," George insisted. As the biggest tattooed guy staggered to an upright position, George swept his leg out, knocking the man's feet out from under him. He fell hard to the floor, cursing.

Dev didn't like leaving his guys, but he needed to get Kiana out of there in case more tattooed gang members showed up.

He grabbed Kiana's hand and left the building, stepping out into the night.

As soon as the door closed behind them, a dark figure leaped out of the shadows and plowed into Dev, slamming him into the wall of the building.

Because Dev had been holding her hand, Kiana was jerked along with him. When he hit the wall, the air was knocked from his lungs, and he released his hold on Kiana's hand.

The man who'd slammed into him grabbed for Kiana.

Dev launched himself at the guy, grabbed the back of the man's shirt and yanked him backward before he could latch onto Kiana. "Run, Kiana!"

When she hesitated, Dev gritted out, "Just go! I'll be right behind you." He spun the man around, shoved him hard into the wall and then ran after Kiana.

He'd only gone a few steps when the man he'd shoved flung himself at Dev, caught him around the waist and knocked him to the ground.

Thankfully, Kiana hadn't stopped.

Sirens blared in the distance, coming closer.

He prayed she'd make it to the car before any more gang members appeared out of nowhere.

The further she got from him, the more worried he became.

Damn it.

He had to get free of this guy and go after Kiana or risk losing her.

WITH THE PARKING lot only a block and a half away, Kiana ran toward it. If she could get to the car, she could drive it to where Dev was fighting yet another gang member. Dev could jump in, and they could get away.

It sounded like a good plan, and it might have worked.

When Kiana was several yards shy of the parking lot, a dark SUV squealed to a stop beside her.

The back door slammed open, and a man jumped out.

Kiana ran faster, reaching the car parking area before the guy caught up to her. She zigzagged between cars, trying to keep one between her and the man chasing her.

When he threw himself over the hood of one and reached for her, she ducked out of reach, rounded the end of a van and dove to the ground. Landing on her belly, Kiana rolled beneath the van and lay still.

Where was Dev? He said he'd be right behind her.

Black boots stopped beside the van.

Kiana rolled away from the boots, out into the open and back beneath the car on the other side of the van. The approaching sirens covered the sound of her movement.

Unfortunately, it masked the sound of her pursuer's movements as well. She'd barely stopped beneath the car when the boots appeared beside her.

Her breath lodged in her throat.

When the man suddenly dropped down beside the car and looked straight into her eyes, Kiana screamed.

A tattooed arm reached beneath the chassis, snagged her leg and dragged her toward him.

As soon as her knees cleared the body of the vehicle, Kiana kicked hard, aiming for the guy's face.

When his grip on her ankle slipped, she rolled back beneath the car and out the other side.

Kiana scrambled to her feet. She made it to the front of the car when the gang member slid across the hood and landed in her path.

He smiled at her, displaying a row of shiny metal teeth. "Bitch, you're coming with me."

"The hell she is," a deep voice said.

Dev appeared behind the man, grabbed his head and slammed it into the hood of the car. The man jerked free of Dev's grip and spun in time to meet a fist slamming into his gut. When he doubled over, Dev brought his knee up sharply, connecting with his face.

The man dropped to the ground and lay still.

Dev grabbed Kiana's hand.

As they ran for the car, Kiana dug the key fob out of her pocket and hit the unlock button. She dove into the passenger seat while Dev jumped into the driver's seat.

Dev drove out of the parking lot, past the man rising from the ground. A dark SUV pulled in front of the exit, blocking their vehicle.

The doors on both sides opened.

The sirens blared loudly. Two police cars raced around a corner a few blocks away, heading straight for the SUV.

The doors slammed shut, and the SUV drove away, stopped briefly at The Big Wave Dive Bar, and then sped away, disappearing around a corner.

The police cars weren't far behind. They sped past the parking lot and ground to a halt in front of the bar.

With their path clear, Dev drove out of the

parking lot and turned away from the bar, the police and the gang that had tried to take Kiana.

She sat quietly in the seat next to Dev, willing her pulse to slow and her breathing to return to normal.

Dev zigzagged through the streets, looking in the rearview mirror. After a while, he slowed, pulled into an alley behind a business and stopped. "I don't think we have a tail." He shifted into Park and looked across at Kiana. "Are you okay?"

She shook her head. "I'm not the one who fought off four gang members. Are *you* okay?"

He nodded. "I'm fine, though I think I gained a few gray hairs when I heard you scream back there."

"About that," she gave him a narrow-eyed glare, "you said you'd be right behind me."

His lips twisted. "I was delayed longer than I anticipated."

She reached for his hand. "Thanks for getting there when you did."

He grinned. "You were doing pretty well on your own."

"I was about to be doing not so well. Your timing was impeccable."

His brow dipped low. "I'm sorry I wasn't right behind you. When that SUV pulled up beside you, I..." His hand tightened around hers. "This evening could've turned out so much worse than it did."

"But it didn't. I'm fine, thanks to you."

"And my team," he said.

She nodded. "I'm worried about your guys. Do you think they made it out all right?"

"I was wondering that myself." He pulled out his cell phone and checked for messages. A grin spread across his face. "George sent a text. They're okay, having a beer at Dukes with Logan. He was sorry he missed the excitement."

Kiana snorted. "I would gladly have missed the excitement."

"George and Rex had every intention of holding onto them until the police arrived, but their reinforcements arrived, three to two became six to two. They had to let them go. An SUV pulled up outside, and they piled in and took off as the police arrived."

"I bet it was the same SUV that blocked our exit." Kiana shook her head. "I wish the police could've arrived before they got away. I'd like to know who sent them."

"Me, too. They seem to be a step ahead or behind our search." He lifted Kiana's hand to his lips and pressed a kiss to the backs of her knuckles. "I'm just glad you're okay. I have to be better at taking care of you. That was too close."

"For all of us." Kiana stared at the hand he still held, the skin tingling where he'd kissed her. As much as she hated to admit it, his kisses in the ladies' bathroom and on the back of her hand had her shaking more than being chased through a parking lot by a tattooed man with silver teeth.

She had to remind herself why she'd sworn off relationships. She couldn't trust her judgment.

All the years in foster care should have hardened her. But there was that little girl deep inside who only wanted to love and be loved. The little girl starving for love made her vulnerable and gullible. Too eager to believe love could last forever when life had proven over and over that it didn't.

Feeling the tempting spark at Dev's touch and staring into his hazel eyes sent her down that slippery slope all over again.

She pulled her hand free of his. "I'd like to go to Meredith and Tish's apartment tonight to see if we can find Meredith's laptop. As unlikely as it might be, I feel we need to rule out Meredith uncovering a rich and evil relative in her search for the family she always wanted."

Dev shifted into drive and pulled out of the alley onto the main road. "I don't feel comfortable going back to the apartment, knowing they're targeting you now. Wouldn't it be better to send George or Rex there to look for your friend's laptop?"

"Trust me. I don't like being targeted either," she said. "I just feel like I need another, slower look at Meredith's things. I know her. Your friends don't. I could notice something out of place that they would completely overlook."

Dev nodded. "True. But I have the feeling whoever attacked you tonight will be watching the apartment for Meredith's return. Or they'll be looking for someone who might know where to find Meredith."

"Then we'll have to sneak into the apartment, look around and get out before we're discovered," she said as brightly as she could when she was still shaking inside at the near-death experiences of the day.

Dev shot a glance her way. "I still don't feel good about taking you back there."

She dipped her head. "Duly noted. However, if you don't take me, I'll get there on my own. I'm going back to the apartment, with or without you."

For a long moment, Dev remained silent.

Kiana would go back to the apartment alone if she had to. But she'd rather have Dev go with her.

He sighed. "I'm taking you to the apartment—against my better judgment."

Kiana let go of the breath she hadn't realized she'd been holding. "Thank you."

While his attention was on the streets in front of him, Kiana studied his profile.

The man was blond, had a strong jaw, a military-short haircut and full, sexy lips. Lips she'd felt against hers.

He was nothing like her ex-fiancé. Looking at Dev, Kiana wondered what she'd ever seen in Carl Brandon.

Sure, Carl was good-looking with his dark hair

and dark eyes. But he'd spent a lot of time in front of a mirror to look that good. He'd had more product for his hair than Kiana had known existed.

Dev, on the other hand, didn't need product to look good. He was naturally, ruggedly handsome. His arms were thickly muscled, and he had a healthy tan from hours spent outdoors.

Carl had acquired his tan at a tanning salon, wanting to make certain it was even all over his body. His arms had never felt nearly as strong as when Dev's had wrapped around her.

She couldn't imagine Dev stealing a woman's life savings to buy a sports car for himself.

Dev glanced at her, his brow wrinkling. "What?"

Kiana was glad it was dark in the car as her cheeks heated. "How do you feel about sports cars?"

He laughed. "They're all right, I guess."

"Have you ever owned one?"

"No." He shrugged. "Never wanted one. I'd rather have a four-wheel-drive Jeep or SUV in case I want to explore roads less traveled. A sports car wouldn't be practical. Besides, I don't like getting down into them and back up out of them. I've always thought guys who owned sports cars had big egos."

"And little dicks," she finished.

Dev laughed out loud. "I didn't say that."

"No. I did."

His eyes narrowed. "Do you know someone with a sports car?"

"I did." Kiana looked away. "We're almost to the apartment. You might want to park a street over. There's another apartment complex before you get to Meredith's. You could park there, and we can walk over."

She guided him into the neighboring apartment complex.

He parked in the shadow of a large trash bin and got out.

Kiana met him at the rear of the car, where he'd popped open the trunk.

He pulled out the shoulder holster, clipped it onto his torso and opened a case containing a handgun. He checked the magazine for live rounds, then shoved the gun into the holster and slipped his arms into a zippered sweatshirt hoodie. The last thing he grabbed was a flashlight. Dev closed the trunk and turned to her. "You have the key to the apartment?" he asked.

She patted her pants pocket. "I do."

He gave a curt nod. "If we're to sneak up on the apartment complex without being spotted, you'll have to follow me and do as I do."

"Yes, sir," she said, her lips twitching. The man was so handsome when he was dead serious. "Lead the way."

He frowned. "This isn't a game."

She touched his arm and nodded. "I know. I wouldn't go back there if I didn't think it was important. We're running out of ideas and people we can question in our search for my friend. I certainly don't want those thugs to find me or Meredith, and I don't want to put you in danger again."

He brushed his thumb across her cheek. "I'm not worried about me. I'm worried I won't be enough to keep you safe."

She captured his hand in hers and turned her face into his palm, pressing her lips to his skin. "You're enough," she whispered, staring up into his blue eyes for longer than she should have. "Come on. Let's do this before I do something stupid."

He chuckled. "Stupid like what?"

Before she could think straight, she rose up on her toes and pressed her lips to his in a brief kiss.

As she dropped back down on her heels, one of his arms came up around her, and his other hand cupped the back of her head, bringing her back to finish the kiss she'd started.

Startled by his move, she gasped.

He took advantage of her parted teeth and darted his tongue in to tangle with hers in a long, slow caress.

Kiana's hands rose from his chest to wrap around the back of his neck, bringing him closer and taking him deeper in a kiss that shouldn't have happened.

For a long, sensuous moment, time stood still. They kissed, and everything else faded into the darkness. Kiana forgot everything but the man in front of her.

When he lifted his head and stared down into her eyes, she had to remind herself to breathe. As she drew in a deep breath, her mind re-engaged, and sanity returned with a vengeance.

Kiana stepped back. "That wasn't supposed to— I shouldn't have— I don't know what got into—"

He covered her mouth with his, stopping her runaway mouth with another kiss that stole her breath away yet again.

When he raised his head this time, she sighed.

"Well, hell." She shook her head. "I can't think."

Dev laughed. "Then don't think. Just feel." He held up a hand. "On second thought, hold those thoughts and feelings until after we're done in Meredith's apartment. We'll revisit them at that time." He took her hand and led her out of the parking lot, across a street and into the shadows of an office building. He paused long enough to say, "Stay close behind me and move in the shadows."

"Yes, sir," she whispered, her pulse ratcheting up the closer they got to the apartment she'd shared with Tish and Meredith. She'd always felt safe in that apartment, surrounded by her friends.

That had all changed in the past few hours. A mental image of Tish flashed through her mind. Her pretty friend lying in the ICU in a coma didn't instill warm fuzzy feelings about returning to the place where she'd been attacked so brutally.

Kiana moved like Dev, clinging to the sides of buildings in the shadows, stopping to check for movement or lurking bad guys. She was determined to get into and out of the apartment without attracting the attention of the men who seemed to be everywhere looking for Meredith or anyone who might know where she was.

Oh, Meredith. Where are you? Why haven't you tried to contact us?

Dev stopped at the corner of the office building across from their destination. The apartment complex lay ahead, bathed in muted starlight with streetlights on each corner.

The abundant lighting had been a selling point when she'd signed the original lease on the apartment years before. All the light made her feel safer. No one could jump out of the shadows to accost her. Now, wanting to enter the apartment undetected, the lights would make it difficult.

Dev spent several long minutes studying the surroundings. "I don't see any sign of movement, but if someone is watching, they'll be doing it from a hidden position. We'll circle behind the furthest cars in the parking lot at the rear of the complex, then move quickly to the door leading into the building. Stay close and move fast."

She nodded. "Will do."

He cupped her cheek and pressed his lips to hers in a brief, hard kiss. "Let's go."

Her lips tingling from his kiss, Kiana followed the Marine, praying they didn't run into any more tattooed gang members.

Enough was enough. They could use a break in this case. Soon. For all they knew, the clock could be ticking for Meredith. Her time could be running out.

CHAPTER 7

DEV LED THE WAY, swinging wide of the building, driveway and parking lot and coming to a halt in the bushes behind the last row of cars. Once they left the bushes, the only cover and concealment would be the vehicles until they reached the building.

So far, Kiana had kept up, matching his movements precisely. She moved with stealth and silence, hunkering low.

His heart swelled at her courage and determination to find her friend. Meredith was lucky she had an advocate in Kiana. She cared about her adopted sisters and had dropped everything in her new life to come back to help them.

In her way, she was like Dev's brothers in arms. She had her sisters' backs. The woman had weathered a foster care system that could have hardened her, yet she still had a heart big enough for everyone with whom she came in contact. She cared what happened to him and his friends.

Dev crouched in the shadows of the bushes, studying the building, the landscaping and the cars parked in front of him. Nothing moved. Short of checking the interior of every vehicle, he couldn't know if someone sat inside one watching for anyone returning to Meredith's apartment.

It seemed a likely scenario. Surely, after a week, she'd want to go back to her apartment, if for nothing else than a change of clothes. If she was on the run, she wouldn't be able to use her credit cards for fear of being tracked by anyone who could hack into a credit card database.

To hide in plain sight, she'd have to eliminate her electronic footprint. A cell phone would be the first loss. Anyone with a bit of hacking experience could get into the phone service database and track her movements.

"See anything?" Kiana whispered behind him.

He brought his thoughts back to the building in front of him. "No. But that doesn't mean there's no one out there." With one hand, he pulled the pistol out of the holster. With the other, he reached for her hand. "Ready?"

"Yes."

He took a deep breath, looked both ways one last time, and then darted across the parking lot, thankful that Kiana had a tall, lithe frame and could keep up with his longer strides.

They made it to the building's back metal staircase without incident and hurried to the second floor.

Though it had only been that morning when they'd been there last, it felt like a lot more time had passed.

Kiana had the key out and ready by the time they reached the door.

Dev twisted the handle. It was locked, unlike their first time there.

Kiana inserted the key and twisted it.

The lock clicked open.

After quietly removing the key, Kiana slipped it back into her pocket. When she reached for the doorknob, Dev blocked her hand and pointed to himself. He motioned for her to stand to the side of the door, then he carefully turned the knob and eased the door open.

The apartment was bathed in darkness, the only light a soft glow streaming through a window from the streetlights.

Dev nudged the door wide enough and then slipped through and to the side, crouching low until he could get his bearings and his eyes could adjust to the limited lighting.

The room appeared as it had when they'd left it

earlier—still a mess from the man who'd gone through it, looking for Meredith and finding Tish.

He reached out for Kiana and pulled her just inside the apartment door, not wanting to leave her standing outside for any longer than he had to.

After a quick and thorough search through the apartment, Dev returned to Kiana. "All clear."

Kiana grimaced. "I don't suppose we could turn on the lights?"

Dev motioned toward the soft light streaming through the window. "If we turn on the light, anyone outside will see it and know someone is inside." He fitted a red lens over the flashlight, switched it on and handed it to Kiana.

She carried the light through the apartment, shining it into corners and spaces. "Meredith worked on her laptop at the little built-in desk in the kitchen." Dev followed her into the compact kitchen with the built-in desk that was more of a cubby hole than a workspace. The desktop had a stack of unopened mail but no laptop.

Kiana moved about the kitchen, opening a drawer full of pens, tacks, paperclips, electrical cords and batteries. She closed it and moved on, checking behind cabinet doors. "I don't think she'd leave her laptop in here, but it doesn't hurt to look." Once she'd opened every door, she left the kitchen and strode through the cramped living area with a small, sectional sofa, a round, glass-topped coffee table and a small flat-screen television propped up on an old dresser.

"When she wasn't at the desk, she would sit on the sofa with her laptop, scrolling through social media, reading the news or listening to self-help podcasts." The end table had been flipped over, its drawer flung across the room.

Dev righted the table and fit the drawer back into its slot. Then he brushed the black powder off his hands from where the police had dusted for fingerprints.

Kiana had already moved into one of the two bedrooms. "Meredith had this bedroom. When Tish moved in, she and I shared a room." She ran her finger along the top of a chest of drawers. "Meredith sometimes took her laptop with her to bed and read late into the night." Kiana tossed aside pillows and looked into the nightstand. She ran her hands between the mattresses on both sides, finding nothing. Getting down on her hands and knees, she peered beneath the bed, finding a box full of memorabilia from Meredith's high school days. Kiana sifted through the contents, finding a photograph of her, Tish and Meredith at a Hawaiian dance class. They stood with their arms draped around each other, colorful leis around their necks and grins spread across their faces.

Kiana remembered that day. It was at the end of a week celebrating Hawaiian culture. They'd each been given a scholarship so that they could attend. They'd learned to hula dance, carve coconuts and weave ribbons and flowers into leis. "What Meredith didn't know about her past, she tried to make up for by saving pieces of her life as she grew up." Kiana had her own box of memories. It wasn't big, but it held cherished items from the happy days of her life.

She sighed and shoved the box back under the bed. When she straightened, she searched the rest of the room for the laptop. It wasn't there. "Do you think the man who attacked Tish got away with the laptop?"

"He didn't have anything in his hands when he leaped off the balcony," Dev said.

Kiana frowned. "It has to be here somewhere unless she managed to get it out before she disappeared." She closed her eyes. "I need to think like Meredith." She opened her eyes and wandered through the room, touching the comforter, the clothes in the closet and a picture frame hung on the wall. In the frame was a photograph of Meredith and her boyfriend, Jason.

Moving back into the living area, Kiana sat on the sofa. She gave a short chuckle. "As creatures of habit, we had our spots. This was Meredith's. We were always digging the remote out from between the arm and the cushion."

Kiana shoved her hand into the gap and frowned. A moment later, she pulled out an electronic tablet with a soft lilac case that opened with a keyboard. She glanced up at Dev. "I've been looking for a laptop. She must have downsized to a tablet."

Kiana touched the button to turn the device on. It blinked, the login screen appeared and then went to black.

"It needs to charge." With the tablet in hand, Kiana jumped up, ran into the kitchen and yanked open the junk drawer. She grabbed a charging cord and plugged it into the wall and the other end into the tablet. This time when she hit the power button, the tablet blinked to life, bringing up a login screen.

"Shoot! What's her password?" Kiana tried Meredith's birthday forward and backward. Tish's birthday. Nothing worked. Then she remembered. "Meredith kept a thin leather journal where she jotted down important information like addresses, account numbers, phone numbers, birthdays...and passwords. Here, hold this." She gave Dev the flashlight.

While he held it, Kiana sifted through the junk drawer. It wasn't there. She ran to the built-in desk, and Dev followed.

One by one, Kiana pulled open the drawers on either side.

About to give up there and check in Meredith's bedroom, she flicked through a stack of blank greeting cards. Tucked beneath was the leatherbound journal. "This is it!"

She opened the journal and leafed through the pages, past information about Meredith's different accounts, friends' birthdays and addresses, finally arriving at the pages full of login IDs and passwords.

Kiana ran her finger down the list, turned the page and continued until she found the one associated with the tablet. "Found it." Right below it was the ID and password for the ancestry site. She looked up at Dev. "And I found the ancestry site login ID and password."

"Is there anything else you need from this apartment?" Dev asked.

Kiana looked around and shook her head. "I think we have what we came for."

"Then let's get out of here before the gang realizes we're here."

A rush of fear sped through Kiana's veins. "Right." She gathered the tablet, the charging cord and the leatherbound journal.

Dev pulled back the curtain hanging over the front window and peered into the parking lot. Out of the corner of his eye, a shadow moved. He focused on the location he thought he'd seen it. All was still. His gut told him it wasn't safe. Staying in the apartment wasn't a good option either.

"Is someone out there?" Kiana whispered behind him.

"I don't know. I thought I saw something move. I could be wrong." He looked back at her. "Let me carry those things. You need to be able to run down the stairs and across the parking lot as fast as you can."

"I can do that and carry this stuff. Besides, you need your hands to be free to hold your gun." Her eyes widened. "Wait here."

She ran into Meredith's bedroom. Moments later, she appeared with a quilted backpack slung over her shoulders. "Now, my hands are free. I'm ready when you are."

He checked out the window once more. When he detected no movement, he eased open the door, pausing long enough to twist the lock. The lock would engage when they closed the door. He shot a glance toward Kiana. "Ready?"

She nodded, her face bathed in the shaft of starlight streaming through the crack in the door.

Dev stepped out, waited for Kiana to clear the door, and then pulled the door closed. He led the way, running down the metal staircase to the ground.

Kiana was right behind him, matching his pace.

Dev had just run out into the parking lot when headlights blinked on. A dark sedan pulled out of a parking space and zoomed straight for him.

Kiana yelled, "Run!"

Dev didn't have time to get out of the way. He waited for the vehicle to reach him and leaped at the last moment. Planting his hands on the hood, he vaulted onto the hood and slid across to the other side.

The sedan rolled past him and Kiana before the driver slammed on his brakes. Doors shot open, and men leaped out.

Kiana ran behind the vehicle, caught up with Dev, and raced for the far side of the lot.

They pushed through the bushes and into the empty lot.

A shout sounded behind them.

Dev ran faster. Kiana stayed at his side but couldn't keep up the pace forever. They had to get to their car or find a place to hide from the men chasing them.

Already, Kiana was slowing. Dev had to think quickly.

They ducked around the back of a small apartment building to an alley with stairs leading up to individual balconies. The wrought iron on one of the balconies had been filled in with a trellis and leafy green ivy, effectively blocking the balcony from the view of passersby.

With no time to spare, Dev grabbed Kiana's hand and raced up the stairs and behind the curtain of ivy. "Duck," he whispered.

Kiana dropped to her haunches, her chest heaving with each ragged breath.

Dev parted a large ivy leaf and stared down at the alley below.

Three men rounded the corner, running fast. They blew through the back alley, passing the apartment building and the trellised balcony where Kiana and Dev hid behind the ivy.

When Kiana started to rise, Dev touched a hand to her back. "Wait."

She lowered to her knees.

A minute later, the three men trotted back through the alley and turned in a different direction.

This time, Kiana didn't try to get up. She stayed where she was.

Dev was fine with staying there for another fifteen or twenty minutes, however long it took to ensure the men had moved on.

A cat climbed the stairs and sniffed at Kiana's hand. After a while, it let her scratch behind its ear, purring loudly. When she stopped scratching, the cat inspected Dev and let him smooth a hand over the cat's soft fur.

A sound in the alley made Dev stiffen. He carefully pulled aside a leaf and peered down to find two of the men walking back through the alley.

The cat chose that moment to meow in protest for Dev having stopped petting the beast before he was ready.

The two men looked up at the balcony.

Dev held his breath.

The cat, having a mind of his own, leaped up onto the bistro table behind Dev.

The two men jumped, their eyes wide.

The taller guy laughed. "It's a goddamn cat."

"What, are you afraid of cats?"

"Hell no," the tall guy said. "Are you? I saw you jump just like me. I don't much like cats. They're creepy."

The other man snickered. "Want me to kill it for you?"

"If you can catch it." The men stared up at the cat.

"Here, kitty, kitty," the short guy called out.

Dev tensed.

The cat didn't move. He wasn't interested in the men down below, being perfectly content on his perch.

The two men started toward the balcony.

Dev bunched his muscles, ready to spring should the men spot him and Kiana.

"Hey, assholes," a gravelly voice shouted below. "They're gone. Let's get out of here."

The shorter guy touched a finger to his temple in salute toward the balcony. "It's your lucky day, cat."

The three men left the alley.

For another five minutes, Dev and Kiana remained crouched on that ivy-screened balcony with the cat keeping watch above them.

"I'm going down first to see if the path to the parking lot is clear," Dev said. "Wait here."

"Nope." She shook her head. "Where you go, I go."

Dev hesitated only a second longer. "You're right.

Come on, we'll make a wide circle to get back to the car."

As they walked through the streets, careful to move in the shadows, Kiana slipped her hand into his.

Eventually, they made it back to the apartment complex where they'd parked the rental car.

Dev held the door for Kiana until she slipped inside.

He rounded to the driver's side and dropped into the seat. "I can't believe it's past midnight. I vote we find a hotel and call it a night. We can look through the tablet there."

"Do you think they know who you are by now?" she asked. "I don't dare use my credit card in case they've hacked into my accounts and can see where I've used the card. Same for you."

"I'll have Hawk reserve a room and let us know where." He called Hawk, feeling bad that he was contacting his boss so late.

"Dev, tell me you and Kiana are okay," Hawk answered.

"We're fine. We went back to Meredith's apartment and found her electronic tablet and password file. We need a place to hole up for the night and don't want to use our credit cards in case they can be traced."

"I'll get right back to you," Hawk said and ended the call.

"He couldn't help us?" Kiana yawned. "It's been a

long day. I'd like to be somewhere safe for the night, so I feel I can close my eyes without worrying we'll have our throats cut in our sleep."

Dev reached out and cupped her cheek. "I won't let that happen."

She laid her hand over his and turned her face to press a kiss into his palm. "What's the plan?"

Dev's phone chirped with a text message. He read it and grinned. "Hank and Sadie have a house on Oahu in a gated community. We're staying there tonight." He hit the pin Hawk had sent, and his map displayed directions from their current location. "First, I think you should turn off your cell phone."

Kiana frowned. "Why?"

"If you're the next target, and they get hold of your cell phone number, they might be able to hack into your phone service and track you by your phone location. Personally, I'd like to sleep tonight without worrying about someone finding us."

Kiana nodded. "This is all assuming whoever is looking for Meredith is smart enough to hack into a phone service's tracking data. But it'd be better to overreact than underreact and get caught." She turned off her cell phone and stared at it for a long moment. "What if she gets to a point where she can call me?"

"She could leave a message."

Kiana shook her head. "I'd hate to miss that call.

But I hate even worse being surprised by that gang again."

Dev held out his cell phone. "If you'll navigate, I'll drive."

"Deal." She took the phone from his hand and repeated what the map application said. Yeah, it was repetitious, but Dev liked hearing Kiana's voice.

"Hank Patterson must be pretty rich to have a house in a gated community," Kiana said.

"Between him and his wife, they do pretty well for themselves," Dev merged onto the expressway, keeping an eye on the rearview mirror for potential tails.

"What's Hank's wife do?" Kiana asked.

Dev laughed. "Ever heard of Sadie McClain?"

Her brow dipped. "Sounds familiar."

"Sadie McClain, the actress?" he prompted, glancing over in time to see her reaction.

Kiana's eyes widened. "*The* Sadie McClain? Hollywood princess, mega-movie star?"

Dev grinned. "That's the one."

"We're staying at her house?"

"Yes, ma'am."

Kiana stared straight ahead. "Wow. I mean... wow."

Kiana missed one of the directions the map app gave.

Fortunately, Dev heard it and made the turn. Soon, they were on a road, climbing up a mountain.

The homes were spaced further apart and were larger and more opulent.

Dev slowed to turn into a gate. A guard met him with an electronic tablet in his hand. "May I help you?"

Dev glanced down at the text message Hawk had sent and read the address to the gate guard.

The guard checked the tablet. "Devlin Mulhaney and Kiana Williams? Could I see some identification?"

Dev and Kiana handed over their driver's licenses.

After a thorough check, the guard handed back the licenses and hit the button to open the gate. "Have a good evening."

Dev rolled up his window and drove through the gate. "I hope the gang that found us at The Big Wave doesn't try to get into this gated community. I doubt one unarmed gate guard could keep them out."

"I was thinking the same thing," Kiana said quietly.

Dev followed the app's directions, winding through the streets and climbing higher up the hillside until the app declared they'd arrive at their destination.

A private drive led to a sprawling modern home with sleek lines of massive glass windows and white stucco glowing in the starlight.

Dev parked to the side of the home in front of a four-car garage.

"How are we supposed to get inside?" Kiana asked.

"Hawk gave me a code for a keypad." He glanced across at Kiana. "Ready?"

"It's almost too beautiful," Kiana said.

"It's amazing on the outside," Dev said. "Let's check it out on the inside." He exited the car and came around to help Kiana out of her seat. Then he opened the trunk, pulled out their small carry-on luggage and set the bags on the pavement. Dev locked the car and pocketed the key.

Since Kiana carried Meredith's electronic tablet and journal, Dev gathered both of their suitcases and carried them toward the front entrance.

At the massive double doors, he found a keypad on the wall and entered the number Hank and Sadie had provided.

The door lock clicked. Dev turned the handle and pushed the door open into a foyer of white marble floors and cathedral ceilings.

"Do they have a security system we need to disarm?" Kiana asked.

"They disarmed it remotely and have it set to reengage after midnight." Dev glanced at his cell phone. "That gives us an hour to explore inside and out before the alarm is set."

"Then we'd better get going. I want to see it all while the tablet is charging." Kiana found an outlet beside a table near the entrance and plugged the tablet into the charger. She laid it and the journal on the table. "It shouldn't take long to charge. In the meantime, let's look around."

Nightlights lit their way through the foyer into a spacious living room with floor-to-ceiling windows overlooking Honolulu and the ocean in the distance. Since they were far up a mountainside, the city lights twinkled below as did the stars above. The view was stunning.

Kiana drew in a deep breath and let it out slowly. "I feel guilty."

Dev left the suitcases in the middle of the living room and came to stand beside Kiana. He slipped an arm lightly around her waist and whispered, "Why?"

She leaned into him. "I'm here, surrounded by beauty and comfort. I'm safe while Meredith is missing, and Tish is lying in a coma in the hospital."

"You're working on helping them," he pointed out, his arm tightening around her. "We're going to find Meredith and the person behind the attacks."

"When?" She turned, rested her hands on his chest and looked up into his eyes. "As far as we know, Meredith has been missing for a week. The clock is ticking, and we still have no clue where she is."

Dev dropped a kiss on Kiana's forehead. "Then let's take a quick tour of the house, raid the refrigerator for something to eat and drink, and then sit down with Meredith's tablet to see what we can find." He kissed the tip of her nose. "Sound like a plan?"

She nodded, her gaze meeting his. "Yes."

Because her face was still tipped up to his, Dev couldn't resist one more...kiss. He brushed his lips across hers in a light touch, not meant to start anything, just to provide comfort.

But once his lips connected with hers, a fire ignited in his groin. It took all his willpower to raise his head.

Kiana's hands slid up his chest, wrapped around the back of his neck and pulled him back down. "Don't start something you can't finish," she whispered and kissed him hard.

When his teeth parted, her tongue slipped past and grazed his in a sexy caress that made his blood burn and his body ache.

When they finally came up for air, Dev cupped the back of her head and breathed against her ear, "Don't start something you can't finish."

She leaned into him, her breasts warm against his chest, his cock pressing into her belly.

God, he wanted this woman. Despite her announcement that she didn't want a relationship and didn't want him to hit on her or fall in love with her, he couldn't help himself. She was smart, feisty, brave and beautiful.

He could easily fall for this woman.

But he was there to help find Meredith, not to break down Kiana's defenses and make love to her.

He set her at arm's length and stared down at her. "My apologies. You did say I wasn't to hit on you."

Her brow furrowed, and she raised her hand to her lips. "I did, didn't I?"

His lips quirked. "I'd say I won't let it happen again, but I can't make that promise. There's something about your lips that I can't resist." He bent and brushed his mouth across hers. "See? Irresistible." He stepped back and let his arms fall to his sides. "Come on. Let's check out this place. It might be the only time I get to stay in a movie star's mansion." He took her hand and led her through the rooms, determined to keep moving. He was afraid that if he stopped, he'd start kissing her again. And, if she let him, he'd keep kissing her. And, oh, the places they could go from there made his blood burn with an unquenchable desire.

Not good. Not good at all.

She'd been quite clear that she wanted none of that nonsense.

Funny, but her words said one thing, and her lips just the opposite.

Yeah. That kiss hadn't been all on him.

She'd wanted it, too.

Dev grinned at the possibilities.

CHAPTER 8

Kiana stood on the balcony outside the master bedroom suite, staring out at the Hawaiian night, wishing her friends were okay and that she could enjoy this setting with no cares in the world.

"Meredith would love this place," she said, reminding herself of her purpose, the reason she'd come back to Oahu.

Dev chuckled. "Hell, who wouldn't? Remind me to thank Hank and Sadie for opening their home to us. And to ask if I can come back when I have more time to swim in the pool and lounge in the hot tub." He leaned on the rail, staring out at the view. "Like you, I feel guilty resting in the lap of luxury when Meredith is still missing, and Tish hasn't woken from the coma." He straightened. "We've seen the house and given the tablet enough time to charge. Let's hope it gives us a clue as to where to look for your friend."

Kiana led the way to the ground floor, where she'd left the tablet charging near the front entrance.

Dev gathered the tablet and charger while Kiana carried the journal. Together, they walked through the living room into the kitchen and laid the items on an island bar.

Dev found another electrical outlet and plugged the tablet in again to keep it charged while they scanned its contents.

Kiana sat on a stool, opened the tablet's case, propped the screen up and laid out the miniature keyboard. Next, she opened the journal and found the page with the passwords. She ran her finger down the list until she found the entry for the tablet and keyed in the login and password. The tablet blinked and displayed the desktop with a tropical beach background.

Dev opened the refrigerator and whistled. "For people who don't come here often, they have a fully stocked refrigerator. What would you like to drink? Beer, wine, a power drink, tea?"

Without looking up, Kiana answered, "Chardonnay, if they have it."

Kiana clicked on icons, one after another until she found Meredith's social media applications and the link that opened the ancestry site. It required another login and password, which she quickly found in the journal. "I'm up on her social media and on the ancestry site."

"Great." Dev set a glass of white wine and a bottle of beer on the counter, walked away and returned with a charcuterie board filled with crackers, different kinds of cheese and olives.

"Nice," she said, and layered a piece of cheese onto a cracker and took a bite. "Mmm. I didn't realize how hungry I was. Not only are you a bodyguard and good in a fight, but you're also handy in the kitchen. What other skills are you holding out on?"

He gave her a sexy smile. "I'm a man of many talents," he said. "I save the best ones for special occasions." Then he winked.

She nearly choked on her cracker as her heart skipped a beat and heat coiled low in her belly.

Kiana wanted to know about the best ones and the special occasions but didn't dare ask. She didn't need to go down that path. Been there, done that, had the empty bank account and broken engagement to prove it.

Still, Dev wasn't Carl. Dev was a man who valued loyalty and honor. Carl only valued himself.

Focus.

She stared down at the tablet until her brain reengaged in the task at hand. Starting with the ancestry site, she bumbled her way through several screens until she came to one with a diagram of people related to each other.

Had Meredith found her blood relatives?

A shiver of excitement rippled through Kiana. Excitement followed by dread. Could one of her blood relatives be the person behind the attacks?

Dev sat on the stool beside her and took a drink of his beer. "My mother is big into genealogy. She tracked her family all the way back to England in the late sixteen-hundreds. She's only gotten my father's line back to Johnson City, Tennessee, in the early eighteen hundreds. But she's still working on it." He leaned close. "What did Meredith find?"

"I'm not sure. It looks like a list of people with similar DNA."

"Not everyone enters data into these programs, but it's surprising how many people do and how much information is available." He pointed to where Meredith's name was displayed. "Apparently, she's found some people she's related to. And if you look at the number of centimorgans shared between her and some other people who've performed DNA testing, she's matched with a number of close relatives.

"Wow." Kiana shook her head. "She must have found this recently. She only got her DNA results back a couple of weeks ago. I haven't gotten mine back yet. After I gifted her the test, she insisted I do it, too. I wonder if she's tried to contact any of these people."

"May I?" Dev asked.

"Please. I'm not sure how to look at all this." Kiana slid the tablet toward him.

Dev scrolled through the list of people whose DNA matched Meredith's. "If this information is current, one of these men could be her father. If you click on each name, you get information that might have been collected on that individual from census reports, birth records, news articles and obituaries. Public records. This man, Robert Pearson, is about the right age to be her father and is considered a close relative."

Dev clicked on Pearson. A disjointed history of his life was displayed. "He graduated from a high school here on Oahu, went to college locally, then attended college in California." He pointed at the screen. "He appears to have stayed in California, moving around a couple of times. He married a woman from California, and they have two children."

"Wow, it's all there." Kiana shook her head. "Except knowing exactly what his relationship is to Meredith."

Dev clicked on the next man, Joe Akana. "This guy is also around the same age as Pearson. He's not related to Pearson at all. They have no matching DNA, which means Pearson could be Meredith's father, and Akana could be related on her mother's side. Or vice versa."

"But she has relatives out there." Kiana stared at the screen, wondering what her DNA test would reveal. Would she find the family she'd longed for all these years? "She just had to untangle the history to find her origin."

"Pretty much." Dev followed the list of entries under Akana. "Born in Honolulu, went to high school here. Married, divorced. He doesn't appear to have had any children of his own. His father was a native Hawaiian, and his mother was an Irish-Hawaiian mix based on her birth parents. Joe had one sister, Martina Akana, two years younger. I'll have Swede search these names." He clicked a couple more times. "Pearson's parents could be grandparents."

"Why doesn't it show the mother?" Kiana asked.

"Probably because she hasn't submitted her DNA to this database," Dev said. "Based on his age, Joe could be a cousin or an uncle."

"He might know who Meredith's mother was, either way."

"True." Dev clicked on the other close relative, someone named Tina M. "This young woman is also a close relative, maybe a cousin or half-sibling."

Kiana's heart squeezed hard in her chest. "A sister?"

"Maybe. But only a *half*-sister."

"Why is only part of her name listed?" Kiana asked.

Dev shrugged. "She might not have wanted her full name released or matched with a birth record."

"Can people contact each other through this

application?" Kiana's brow furrowed. "How frustrating would it be if you found a match and couldn't contact that person?"

"People can send messages through the app," Dev said. "The receiver can choose to respond or not."

"Is there a way to see the history of those messages?" Kiana asked.

"Let me check." Dev clicked through several screens until he found where Meredith had initiated messages to some of the people identified as close relatives.

Kiana leaned closer. "Did any of them respond?"

"Nothing from the Pearson or Akana." Dev brought up a message Meredith had sent to Tina M. "That's odd. It appears as if Tina responded and then deleted her response, so you can't read what she had to say to Meredith."

Kiana sighed. "Well, at least we have a few names we can check."

Dev pulled out his cell phone. "I'll text those names to Swede. It'll be too early in the morning to call because of the time difference between Hawaii and Montana." While Dev sent the text message with the names of the two men, Kiana left the ancestry app and switched over to Meredith's social media.

Kiana knew a lot of the people Meredith connected with on social media because they'd had the same friends and jobs for so long. Kiana had the new friends she'd made on Maui, and Meredith had some Kiana didn't recognize. She went through those first, looking for any individual messages she might have exchanged. Nothing stood out until she came to a friend whose name appeared as T. Mercer.

Several messages had been exchanged between Meredith and T. Mercer.

"What did you find?" Dev asked.

"I'm not sure." Kiana studied the messages. "This person and Meredith have been messaging each other quite a bit."

Kiana scrolled back further to find a message from Meredith telling T. Mercer she was a model when she could get the work. Before that, she'd asked T. Mercer what she did for a living. T. Mercer had responded that her health kept her from working outside the home. She did some work editing term papers for college students.

"Apparently, T. Mercer lives with her father and doesn't get out much because of health issues. She sounds lonely." Kiana smiled. "Meredith has a big heart. She probably kept her company online." Kiana scrolled down, her chest tightening. "It's sad because for the last few days, T. Mercer has messaged the word 'Hello' several times, and Meredith hasn't responded."

"It's getting late," Dev said. "We should get some rest."

"I know. I need to keep up my strength to help my friend." Kiana closed the tablet case, rose from the bar stool and stretched. "I suppose the alarm system was set already. I would've liked to step outside once more before going to sleep."

"We can look out the windows," Dev offered. "It's almost as good as going outside. The view is the same." He held out his hand.

Kiana placed hers in his, knowing it might be a mistake, but she was too tired to care. She liked how firm and strong his hand was.

He led her to the windows and stood beside her as she stared out at the city lights below and the stars above. "The view is beautiful," she said softly.

Dev chuckled. "But—"

"When we were out on the balcony, I could smell the plumeria blossoms." She gave him a twisted smile. "It adds another dimension to the magnificence of Hawaii."

He brushed a strand of hair back from her cheek, tucking it behind her ear. "We'll be sure to start the day on the balcony tomorrow."

She smiled up at him. "I would like that." Her smile faded. "Do you think we'll find Meredith? What if something terrible happened to her, and she's disappeared forever?" Kiana closed her eyes. "I never should've left Oahu. My sisters needed me, and I abandoned them."

Dev's hands cupped her cheeks. "Look at me, Kiana."

She opened her eyes and stared into his.

"You can't blame yourself for what's happening. You didn't hurt Tish. The man who attacked her did that. Even if you still lived with them, you might not have been home when he broke in. And if you had been home, he could've hurt both of you. Then, who would've searched for Meredith."

Tears welled in her eyes. "Poor Tish. How terrifying it must have been. And Meredith... We have no idea what's happening to her." A sob rose in her throat as tears spilled from her eyes.

"Oh, babe, don't," Dev said, brushing away the tears with his thumbs. "I can take a beating any day, but tears...they destroy me." He kissed one eye, then the other.

The tears slowed to a stop as Kiana's breath caught and held.

When his kisses moved to her lips, she melted into him, grateful for his solid strength and compassion—and so much more.

He made her forget that there were bastards out there like her ex-fiancé who had no moral compass. Dev made her believe that maybe, just maybe, love was real, not just some stupid fairytale existing only in books.

Even if it wasn't love that she was feeling, she didn't want it to stop. Not yet. At that moment, what she felt was the only thing keeping her afloat in a sea of sadness and despair.

For a fraction of time, she chose to forget the

heavy burden of uncertainty and bask in the certainty of the heat burning through her body, warming her from her core to the very tips of her being.

When Dev raised his head, Kiana moaned.

"If I don't stop here," he whispered against her ear, "we're headed down a path you didn't want."

"Don't," she said past the breath lodged in her throat. "Don't stop. I need your arms around me, your body against mine." She clasped his face in her hands. "I need to feel everything that reminds me I'm alive." She kissed him hard, thrusting her tongue past his teeth to feel his warmth and taste his essence.

He thrust back, taking as well as giving, claiming her mouth as his.

Again, his lips left hers, and she almost cried out as if in pain.

Dev bent, scooped her up into his arms, and carried her through the beautiful living room. He didn't stop until he crossed the threshold into the master bedroom. When he lowered her legs to the floor, she leaned into him, pressing her breasts to his chest while wishing they were already naked.

Her hands rose to grab the hem of his shirt, dragging it up his torso, over his chest and head. Once she'd freed him of his shirt, she tossed it aside and went to work on the button securing the waistband of his jeans.

When her fingers fumbled, he brushed her hands

aside, slipped the button loose, dragged down his zipper and let his cock spring free.

Kiana grasped him in her hands, amazed and completely turned on by how long, thick and hard he was.

He tipped her chin up and stared down into her eyes. "You have to tell me what you want, or this stops here."

His cock twitched in her palm. She licked dry lips and swallowed. Then she released her hold on his shaft, gripped the hem of her shirt and pulled it up over her head, tossing it to the side. "I want you. Inside me. Now."

He tipped his head slightly. "Are you sure?"

She reached behind her back and unhooked her bra, letting the straps slide from her shoulders. With a wicked grin, she stood in front of him, naked from the waist up. "Positive."

"No regrets?" he persisted.

"My only regret is that you're stalling." Her eyes narrowed. "If you don't want this…" Her eyes widened. "Wow…I just assumed."

He chuckled and gripped her arms. "I want this more than I want to breathe. I just want you to be sure it's what you want. You're hurting and upset. You might not be thinking straight. If all you need is someone to hold you, I can do that." He let out a tight breath. "It'll be hard, but I'll hold you, and we don't have to go any further than that."

She pressed a finger to his lips. "Shut up."

"You said you didn't want me to hit on you."

"Shh." Kiana shook her head, remembering the words she'd spoken when they'd been on Maui. "All of that stands. I don't want a relationship. I'm not good at those. All I want is tonight. You haven't hit on me. I believe we find each other mutually attractive, and there's nothing wrong with exploring that chemistry. As long as we both agree there are no strings attached." She met his gaze, arching an eyebrow.

He hesitated, his lips pressing together.

For a long moment, Kiana thought he'd decline her offer.

"Okay," he finally said. "No strings. One night and no promises."

She nodded, confused by the disappointment niggling at the back of her mind. What had she expected? She'd come up with the rules. Dev had only agreed with them.

Without a fight.

Some of the heat fizzled as she stood with her naked skin chilled by the breeze from the air conditioner.

He gave her a crooked smile, his hands still resting on her arms. "How do we pick up from here?"

She laughed nervously. "I don't know. Did we spoil the mood by talking too much?" She swayed toward him. "Maybe if we...kissed." Leaning up on her toes, she pressed her lips to his.

At first, he didn't respond.

Kiana almost cried in frustration. Inside, she was still burning for his touch. Had he lost his desire?

Then his arms rose around her, gathering her close. His hard cock pressed against her soft belly. No. His desire hadn't cooled.

Kiana ran her hands down his back to the waist-band of his jeans and slid them beneath to cup his firm ass in her palms. She spoke against his lips. "Is it me, or are we moving too slow?"

"Too slow," he gritted out. He set her at arm's length, dug for his wallet in his back pocket, pulled a condom packet from inside and placed it between his teeth. Then he jammed his wallet into his back pocket and shucked his jeans, kicking his shoes and the jeans to the side.

Kiana toed off her shoes and shimmied out of her slacks.

They stood before each other, Dev naked, Kiana wearing only the lace thong panties she'd started the day in.

Dev handed Kiana the condom packet, then scooped her up gently in his arms and carried her to the king-sized bed.

At five-feet-ten, Kiana was thin but no light-weight. Yet, Dev carried her as if she weighed nothing.

He laid her on the duvet and stepped back for a second, his gaze sweeping over her from her eyes to her toes. "You're beautiful," he said in a raspy voice.

If Carl had stood looking at her like Dev was now, Kiana would have felt self-conscious. He'd always found something not quite right with her appearance and hadn't hesitated to point it out.

The way Dev looked at her didn't make her want to hide her imperfections. His gaze worshipped every inch of her, coming back to her eyes.

He stretched out beside her, leaning up on his elbow. "Tell me what you like," he said.

She trailed her finger down his chest. "Surprise me with your special talents," she said, her voice husky with a desire so strong that she wanted to throw him on his back, mount him and take all of his stiff shaft inside.

He leaned over her, his lips hovering over hers. "Prepare to be ruined."

She chuckled. "Overly confident?"

"Just honest." He pressed his lips to hers and made love to her mouth. By the time he came up for air, she was squirming beneath him, ready for so much more than a kiss.

As he worked his way down her body, tasting and touching, Kiana realized she was in trouble.

He took his time and made her feel as if there wasn't a single inch of her that he hadn't set on fire.

She writhed beneath him, moaning.

He was right.

Everything he did to her ruined her for any other man.

She was afraid. Terrified. What if she didn't want this to end? What if she wanted him to keep going on forever? She'd set the limit. One night.

Holy hell. One night would never be enough.

CHAPTER 9

DEV LOVED how Kiana came alive at his touch. He treasured all of her, taking his time getting to know her body, her erogenous zones and everything that made her moan.

He stopped to feast on her breasts, sucking the tips deep into his mouth, flicking the nipples until they hardened into tight little beads. They were perfect, filling his hands full of her dark flesh. Her skin was soft beneath his lips and tongue.

Moving lower, he pressed kisses to each of her ribs as he worked his way down her torso, inch by inch.

By the time he reached the juncture of her thighs, her breath had grown ragged. Her fingers roved his body in jerky, frenetic movements, as if she was holding back but didn't want to.

His cock was so hard, it hurt, but he wanted to

bring her all the way to orgasm before he considered slaking his own desires.

He'd promised to ruin her. He'd stop at nothing less. He wanted her to know what making love should feel like: the rush of emotion, the burning passion and wild abandon it inspired. Any other man would fall short of what Dev would elicit from Kiana.

He was driven to accomplish this goal. For a moment, he wondered why. She'd been so insistent that she wanted nothing to do with a relationship.

Did he see her declaration as a challenge? If so, what did he hope to gain? Did she really only want a night of hot sex and the following day pretend it never happened?

No. Dev shook his head. He didn't work that way. He wanted more than a quick tumble in bed. After sacrificing his life and any decent relationship for the military, he wanted a home, a woman to share his bed and let him hold her naked body against his for as long as they both lived.

If Kiana was that woman, he'd have to really work to convince her to give him a chance.

When he parted her folds, she reached for his head.

His hair was too short for her to gain purchase. Instead, she massaged his scalp, urging him closer, eventually grasping his ears, tugging gently, encouraging him to touch more, take more.

Dev chuckled, blowing a stream of warm air

across her sex. With slow, methodical patience, he flicked her clit with the tip of his finger, repeating the motion and adding other tricks of his touch to drive her wild.

Her body rocked beneath him, responding to each flick. When he touched his tongue there, she gasped.

"Oh, Dev…that's…that's…"

He swirled his tongue around that nubbin of flesh.

"That's soooo good," she breathed.

While he tongued her clit, he slid a finger into her moist channel, then another.

Her body tensed, and her back arched off the mattress. "Yes!" she cried. "Oh, sweet beaches, yes!"

Dev didn't slow, didn't let up, powering through his campaign to ruin her for any other man.

Her hips rocked with her release until she dropped back to the mattress, breathing hard. Her skin was so soft, her muscles taut, her long hair splayed out across the pillow. God, she was beautiful, passionate and his for the night.

Dev smoothed a hand along the inside of her thighs. "Like that?"

"Mmm," she said. "It was good…for a start."

He chuckled as he climbed up her body, settling his hips between her legs. "That was just the teaser."

She smiled up at him. "You mean there's more to come?"

He bent to take her lips in a long, sensuous kiss.

Kiana wrapped her fingers around the back of his neck and returned the pressure, her calf wrapping around his thigh, making it harder for him to maintain control.

He was so hard and ready that he was afraid he'd come too soon.

Dev broke the kiss and patted the mattress, searching for the condom packet he'd thrown onto the bed earlier.

Kiana's hand slipped beneath her back and pulled out the packet. "Looking for this?"

When he reached for it, she shook her head.

"Uh-uh. My turn." She arched an eyebrow in challenge.

He grinned and kissed the tip of her nose. "Okay. Just know, I'm so close now, I'm ready to explode."

"I'll just have to hurry." She planted her hands against his chest and rolled him over onto his back. Then she straddled his hips and bent to kiss him.

But only for a brief second before she skimmed her lips across his chin and down the side of his neck to the base, where his pulse thundered in his veins.

He rested his hands on her hips, wanting to raise her up and bring her down over his aching dick.

Her lips, her tongue, her body against his was driving him insane with desire.

But she wasn't done. Her lips trailed across his collarbone, captured one of his nipples and sucked gently. Moving lower, she scraped her fingernails softly town his torso, kissing a path to his turgid cock...hard, thick and ready.

Sitting back on her haunches, she wrapped her hands around his shaft and slowly stroked him up and down. When Kiana leaned forward and took him into her mouth, it was all Dev could do to keep from coming.

He tensed, fighting for control.

Her mouth moved to cover him, taking him in. She lowered her head, cupped his balls and sank down until all of him was inside her mouth, bumping against the back of her throat. She lifted her head until he came out all the way to the tip. Her tongue traced around the head and then she took him again, all the way into her mouth.

Dev tensed, his insides an inferno ready to explode.

What she was doing was sweet heaven.

Dev cupped the sides of her face and lifted her off him. "I can't hold back another second."

She nodded, tore open the packet and rolled the condom over his cock. Then she straddled him and lowered herself until he slid into her hot, wet channel.

Kiana's eyes closed as she threw back her head and sank down on him, taking all of him inside.

He gripped her hips and held her in place, allowing her to adjust to his thickness.

Her head came up, and her gaze locked with his as

she rose until he almost slipped free. With a sexy smile, she held him at the edge for a moment, then dropped down.

Dev guided her into a rhythm, up and down, faster and faster, until he was right on the edge of his release. Stopping suddenly, he lifted her off.

In a swift movement, he rolled her onto her back and leaned over her.

She reached between them and directed his cock to her entrance.

Dev eased into her, loving the way her channel contracted around him.

"So good," she whispered.

Once he was fully seated, he eased out and back in. Again. And again. The urgency of his need accelerated the pace until he was pumping in and out like a piston in an engine.

Kiana raised her knees, pushing her heels against the mattress, meeting his every stroke.

He tensed. The intensity of sensations shot him over the edge. Dev plunged deep into Kiana and remained buried as his cock pulsed with wave after wave of his release.

When the waves subsided, he dropped down onto Kiana and kissed her long and hard.

She wrapped her legs around him, holding him close.

Concerned that he was crushing her, he rolled them onto their sides and pulled her in his arms.

"You were right," she whispered, her breath warm against his chest.

He brushed a strand of her hair from her face. "About what?"

"You do have special talents."

"That was just the main show," he said, brushing a kiss across her forehead. "Wait until you experience the finale and the encore."

"Mmm," her sound hummed against his skin, reigniting the fire in his veins. "So, this is inter-mission?"

"Babe." He kissed her temple. "That was only Act I. This show can go on for as long as you have hours in the day, days in the week and weeks in the year... You get the picture? I'm not just good at a sprint; I'm also good for distance and endurance."

She chuckled. "We're mixing metaphors."

"I'm also good at mixing drinks," he moved over her and pressed his lips to the base of her neck where her pulse beat wildly. "Like Sex on the Beach, Slip-pery Nipple and..." He laughed. "Point is my talents guarantee never a dull moment and always a good time." He brushed kisses across her collarbone and downward to take one of her nipples into his mouth.

He couldn't get enough of her. Even if he wasn't up to the next round yet, he loved making her come. If tonight was the only chance he got to be this close to her, he could sleep another day.

Ever the optimist, Dev refused to believe this was

a one-night stand. He wanted a lifetime of nights and days with this amazing woman. Once was not enough.

TRUE TO HIS WORD, Dev showed Kiana Act II, a finale and encore before she dropped into an exhausted and sated sleep.

The irritating chirp of a cell phone woke her far too soon. When she reached for her phone, she realized it wasn't hers that was ringing.

"Hey, Swede… No, I was awake. What have you found?"

Kiana rolled over to find Dev sitting on the edge of the bed, his naked back to her.

Her blood stirred at her core. Even after making love until the early morning hours, she wanted to do it again.

With Dev.

He made her feel special, alive, totally feminine and powerful all at once. He knew exactly where to touch her to bring her the most pleasure and took his time to make sure she was satisfied before he pleased himself.

Carl had never bothered to ask Kiana what she wanted when it came to sex. Sex had been all about him. She'd even faked orgasms to stroke his ego.

With Dev, every orgasm had been the real deal.

His fingers, tongue and…well, everything he touched her with was magic.

Kiana smiled, realizing this was what making love should be. Sharing the intimacy, the work, the play and learning about your partner's wants and needs.

Damn. Dev had been right again. His lovemaking had ruined her.

For anyone else.

She couldn't even imagine another man eliciting the kind of passion Dev had inspired in her. Hell, she didn't want to think of anyone but Dev touching her, kissing her, looking at her naked body the way he did.

"Can you shoot me Akana's address? We'll swing by his place this morning. And give Pearson's phone number. We'll call him. I don't see flying over to California to meet with him face to face unless we have to." Dev listened for a moment. "Yeah, if you find anything on Tina M, send it our way as well…" Dev nodded. "Right. I'll get those to you ASAP. Thanks. Out here." He ended the call and turned to Kiana.

"Swede?" she asked.

"Yeah." He set the phone on the nightstand and laid down beside Kiana, pulling her into his arms. "He found Joe Akana here on Oahu. He's texting his address. He located Pearson in Los Angeles. We'll get his phone number. He's still trying to figure out who Tina M is. He wants whatever login and passwords Meredith used for social media and the ancestry application. He can dig deeper than we can."

"Normally, I wouldn't dream of sharing her passwords," Kiana said. "But if it helps us find Meredith, I'll do it."

Dev pulled her close until their bodies were pressed firmly together. His hard cock pressed into Kiana's belly. "Isn't it too early to visit Joe Akana?" She kissed the base of his throat and flicked the pulse beating there with her tongue.

"Absolutely," he agreed and swept his hand over her hip, cupping her ass.

She stilled. "What if Akana goes to work early? We might miss him."

"Not a chance," Dev said. "Swede says he's on social security for a back injury he received on the job fifteen years ago. I doubt he's going anywhere early in the morning. I figure we have another hour to sleep or whatever."

Kiana's hand slipped down Dev's flat belly to circle his arousal. "I vote for whatever."

They spent the next thirty minutes whatevering until they both were thoroughly satisfied. For the moment.

They lay side by side, recovering from their workout when Dev's stomach rumbled.

When Kiana's echoed in response, she pressed her hand to her stomach and laughed. "Food might be a good idea.

He sat up immediately. "I'm glad you said that. I wasn't going to mention it until you did."

She frowned. "Why were you waiting for me?"

"I didn't want you to think I couldn't go the distance." He winked and slapped her bare ass playfully. "Come on. I saw eggs in the refrigerator and a coffeemaker. We can be fed and on the road in no time."

"Take me to your coffee machine," she said and rolled out of the bed. She walked naked across the room, using her modeling strut. When she stopped to look over her shoulder to gauge Dev's reaction, she was startled to find him directly behind her. "Geez, how did I not hear you move?"

He grinned. "SEAL training." His hands settled on her hips, pulling her back against his hard cock. "I couldn't resist the sway of your hips." He nuzzled the side of her neck, his hands smoothing up her torso to cup her breasts.

She leaned back, giving him better access to kiss her cheek. "Mmm. I could skip the eggs as long as I can take a cup of coffee to go."

Dev turned her in his arms. "I could make love with you all day."

Kiana sighed. "I do like the sound of that, but..."

"We need to find your friend."

She nodded. "A shower, eggs and coffee. Then we hit the road. I hope Mr. Akana has some information that will help."

Kiana dressed quickly, stealing glances at Dev as he pulled on his jeans.

The man had a beautiful body, with not an ounce of fat anywhere to be seen. And she'd seen it all. Her core still radiated with the heat he'd stirred inside her.

She'd never felt this sexually excited with any other man she'd been with. Not that she'd been with many. Carl had been her longest relationship. They'd been together for three years.

Even after he'd asked her to marry him, he'd insisted they maintain separate residences until they married, which had made it easier for him to end the engagement. She hadn't had to move her things out of his apartment. She'd only left a few articles of clothing, a toothbrush and some cosmetics there for when she'd stayed the occasional night.

Carl had shipped her things in a box without taking time to make sure her cosmetics wouldn't leak or break. The box had arrived with a broken bottle of lotion spilled over one of her favorite blouses. She'd tossed it all in the trash. That night, she'd applied for a job on Maui at the resort; the next day, she'd gotten the call to interview. She'd packed everything she'd owned into two suitcases, left her furniture to Tish and Meredith and had moved to Maui, determined to stay whether she got the job or not.

That had been over two years ago. She hadn't dated, hadn't wanted to and had kept men at arm's length.

"I'll get the coffee brewing while you're finishing up in here," Dev said and left the room.

Kiana's gaze followed him out the door as she worked the tangles out of her long hair with the brush she'd brought with her. She quickly twisted her long hair into one long braid down her back. After she pulled on her shoes, she grabbed her purse and followed her nose to the kitchen and the coffee.

"Scrambled or fried?" Dev asked with two eggs in his hands, poised over a small skillet.

"Scrambled," she said and made a beeline to the coffeemaker.

"I found a loaf of bread in the freezer and popped a couple of pieces into the toaster." As if on cue, the toast popped up. "I timed that announcement perfectly." He set the toast on a small plate next to the stove.

Kiana grinned and maintained her vigil over the coffee pot. When the last drop fell into the carafe, she poured two cups of the steaming brew and carried them over to where Dev stirred fluffy yellow eggs around in the pan.

"Did you want milk or sugar in yours?" she asked as she held out a mug to him.

"No way." He took the coffee and inhaled the steam. "I like mine hot and black. No frills."

"Me, too." She sipped, careful not to burn her tongue.

He grinned over the rim of his mug. "You're not a caramel latte with whipped cream kind of girl?"

She shrugged. "I do like dessert coffee on occasion, but as a model, every calorie counted. I learned to drink black coffee and prefer it that way now."

Dev nodded. "When you're in the field with limited rations, you take what you can get."

His mention of life in the field made Kiana realize how little she knew about this man. "What was it like being a Marine?"

Dev set the mug of coffee on the counter and stirred the eggs in the pan once more. "These eggs are ready." He tipped the pan over a plate and scraped half the eggs out before depositing the rest on the second plate, adding toast to each.

As she carried her plate to the bar stool, Kiana figured Dev didn't want to talk about his time in the military. She wasn't going to push the issue, though she really wanted to know more about him.

Dev sipped his coffee and took up his fork. "Being a Marine was perhaps the best and the worst time of my life."

Kiana was surprised by his words but hid the surprise by popping a forkful of eggs into her mouth. If he wanted to expand on his statement, he would. If not, she'd respect his desire to keep his thoughts to himself.

He chewed on some eggs and swallowed before he spoke again. "The training was hard, physically and mentally. There were times I didn't think I'd make it—not from lack of trying but from my body's reaction to the stress. I learned that I could do things

I didn't initially think possible. I learned to rely on my teammates. I also learned that if you hang in there long enough, the bad stuff will pass."

"Was that the worst part of your life?" she asked softly.

He snorted. "Not actually. It was hard, but coming out of it, I've never been so thankful and proud to be Marine Force Recon."

She lifted her coffee mug and asked casually, "What was the worst part of being Marine Force Recon?"

He stared down at the food remaining on his plate. "Holding one of my Marine brothers in my arms as he bled out from a shrapnel wound. Watching the helicopter next to yours explode, killing every soul on board. My teammates, my brothers. Coming home to the States to find your wife has sold all your shit, taken your kids and left you for a goddamn insurance salesman."

Kiana's brow furrowed. "Your wife left you?" She hadn't thought to ask him if he was married, divorced or single.

Dev met her gaze. "No, but I watched too many of my buddies' marriages fall apart because they were never home. One of my friends, Mack, came back from a really shitty deployment where we lost half the men on our team. He went to his house and found some other family living there. His wife had left him, took his two kids and moved in with another man."

"The insurance salesman?" she asked.

Dev nodded. "It was the straw that broke Mack. He went out to the beach where we'd done our BUDs training, watched the sunset and blew his brains out."

Kiana's stomach roiled. She swallowed hard to keep from losing the few bites of eggs she'd just consumed. When she could speak again, she reached out and touched Dev's arm. "I'm sorry."

He shrugged. "Sometimes, I think he took the easy way out. Life is hard enough when you're dodging bullets and getting hit with shrapnel, but those are physical pains. When the person who's supposed to love, honor and cherish you shoots you in the back, how do you recover from that?" He shook his head. "It's hard to go back to work after something like that."

"Is that when you decided to leave the Navy?"

"The whole chain of events contributed to my decision, but Mack's suicide sealed it for me. We'd lost so many of our team, to lose one more..." Dev stared at his hands.

Kiana's heart pinched hard in her chest. She wished she could take away this man's pain but knew she couldn't.

"The team wasn't the same," he said. "I'd lost my stomach for war and death." For a long moment, he sat looking at his plate. Then he glanced up. "We're not getting any closer to finding your friend sitting around here while you're listening to my sob story. Let's go talk to Joe Akana."

"Before we go," Kiana said, "what's Swede's email address?"

Dev texted Swede for the information. Once Kiana had the email address, she forwarded the logins and passwords for the ancestry site and Meredith's social media, making a note to look for Tina M. and T. Mercer on Meredith's social media since T. Mercer had been her most recent conversation. Once done, she closed the laptop.

Having been fortunate enough to use Hank and Sadie's vacation home, Kiana and Dev wanted to leave it like they'd found it. Clean and beautiful.

Kiana washed dishes while Dev dried, thinking about Dev's losses and comparing them to hers. Losing Carl had been nothing. She'd suspected she hadn't really been in love with the man but more in love with the idea of having someone in her life.

She'd realized then that she had people in her life who cared about her. Even if her mother had abandoned her, she had her sisters, Meredith and Tish. And, like Dev, the thought of losing them was too much to bear.

Damn it.

She had to think positive. Tish would get better. With Dev's help, they'd find Meredith, come hell or high water.

CHAPTER 10

FOR THE FIRST fifteen minutes of the drive to Joe Akana's place, Dev wallowed in the black cloud he hadn't allowed himself into for a while. Talking about what had happened on his last mission with his Marine Force Recon team and Mack's subsequent suicide brought back the heaviness he'd experienced at the time.

The overwhelming feeling of doom that had plagued him for months and had made him walk away from the only job he'd ever known and loved returned in full force.

"Hey." Kiana touched his arm. "I'm sorry if I brought back bad memories."

Dev shook his head in an attempt to climb out of the darkness the memories brought with it. He was in Hawaii with a beautiful woman he'd made love to all night long. If he'd learned one thing, life did get better after the bad times. He needed to focus on the good times back then and the good things to come. "It's okay. I can't change the past or bring back the people I lost, but I can remember their spirit, the good times and how much we cared about each other. I lived for a reason. Not to repeat the past, but to forge a new future."

"Helping others," Kiana added with a gentle smile. "Like me and Meredith."

He nodded, hoping he did manage to help her and her friends. They hadn't gotten very far with what they knew. Joe Akana needed to give them something they could sink their teeth into.

They entered a neighborhood that had seen better days. The houses were dilapidated, needing to be stripped of their peeling paint and repainted. Some should have been torn down and rebuilt.

What they found at the address they'd been given wasn't much of a house but more like a hut of tin, plywood and concrete blocks. Metal chairs stood on what could loosely be called a porch with a sagging deck and an equally sagging, corrugated tin awning.

As Dev pulled into the gravel driveway and shifted into Park, a grizzled man with dark skin and graying hair pushed the torn screen door open and leaned against the rotting doorframe. "Don't bother getting out," he called out. "Ain't buyin' nothin'. Ain't got no money, anyway."

Kiana was out of the car before Dev. "We're not

selling anything," she said with a smile. "Are you Mr. Joe Akana?"

"Don't know about the Mr., but yeah, I'm Joe. Who wants to know?"

"I'm Kiana Williams," she said. "I'm looking for a friend and hoped you could help."

"Don't know how. I'm sure I don't know your friend." He lumbered across the rotting deck and eased into one of the metal chairs. "You're wasting your time."

"I really hope I'm not wasting my time, Mr. Akana." Kiana stepped closer. "My friend might be in danger, and I'm not sure where to turn."

He looked past Kiana to Dev. "Your boyfriend not helping?"

Her cheeks turned a pretty shade of pink. "He's helping by being my bodyguard. Some dangerous people have already hurt others looking for my friend. I need to find her before they do. Please, Mr. Akana, could I ask you some questions? I'd really appreciate it, and it might help us figure out where to look."

The older man shrugged. "Don't know what I'd have to say that could help, but since you asked all nice like, I guess it won't hurt."

"Thank you," she said and walked closer to the porch.

"Got another chair up here," he said. "Have a seat." To Dev, he shook his head. "Sorry. I only got the one."

"That's okay." Dev dipped his head. "It won't hurt me to stand."

"Nice that you can," Akana said. "Hurt my back several years ago. Can't stand for long without it causing me a lot of pain."

Dev wasn't happy when Kiana climbed the rickety stairs to the porch. The stairs, the deck and the awning looked like a stiff wind could blow them away.

Kiana took the seat beside Akana and gave him a tight but friendly smile. "My friend Meredith and I both grew up in the foster care system. She's always wanted to know her birth family."

Akana snorted. "Hoping she could find a rich daddy so she can claim his inheritance?"

Kiana shook her head. "No. Meredith doesn't care about the money. She just wants to know where she came from, the people who made her and who she is. Her roots. In the foster care world, you don't have anyone you can call family. Like me, she was passed from home to home." Kiana stared down at her hands. "People who know who their parents are can say, I got my blue eyes from my father and my red hair from my mother. They can trace hereditary diseases to family members and stay ahead of health issues."

"What does all that have to do with me?" Akana asked.

"She did one of those DNA tests and joined an

ancestry application that links people to others with similar DNA."

Akana snorted. "I did one of those DNA tests. Told me what I already knew. I'm mostly of Hawaiian, Pacific Islander descent." He tilted his head to one side. "What I didn't know was I had a bit of Irish in me." He waved his hand at his face. "Who would think that, looking at me? Except for my green eyes."

Kiana hadn't noticed until that moment that Joe's eyes were green.

"I got the green eyes; Martina didn't." He thumped his chest. "No matter. I'm Hawaiian, through and through. Like you. Your genes show in your face, your hair and your heart."

Kiana nodded. "I can't deny my heritage. I took one of those tests as well. I just haven't seen the results yet. My friend Meredith got hers and found several people who are considered close relatives based on the amount of matching DNA. You were one of them."

Akana's eyes narrowed. "Me? I just did the test to learn about my heritage, not to look for relatives. What would she want with me? I'm not rich. I got nothing to give to your friend."

"We saw that you have a sister," Kiana said.

"Huh," Akana said. "*Had* a sister. She could've been anything. Smart, pretty, popular in school." He shook his head. "Got mixed up with an older guy when she was sixteen. Ended up pregnant. Our parents kicked her out of the house. They told her to get her boyfriend to man up and take care of her and the baby."

Kiana leaned toward the man, her gaze intense. "Do you know what year that was?"

Akana closed his eyes and tilted his head. "I was a senior in high school. Must've been around thirty or thirty-one years ago." His eyes narrowed. "Why? Do you think my sister was your friend's mother?"

Kiana sank back in her chair, shaking her head. "Meredith was abandoned as an infant. She's only twenty-eight years old."

"That wasn't the only kid my sister had," Akana said.

"No?" Kiana sat up straighter.

"Several years after my parents kicked her out, she showed up at my apartment. She wanted me to help her. She said she was pregnant and had nowhere to go. I had a roommate. I couldn't let her live with me, especially if she was going to have a baby. I was working at my first job in a warehouse and barely made enough to pay my half of the rent. I told her to go to our parents. She shook her head and said they wouldn't speak with her."

Kiana's hand pressed to her chest.

Dev could tell she was upset for the young teenager whose parents had turned their backs on her when she'd needed them most. He wanted to go to Kiana and hold her. The woman had a big heart that extended to a woman she didn't even know.

Akana continued. "I asked her what happened to her boyfriend and the other baby. She said that her boyfriend had left Hawaii over a year before, saying he'd be back for them. But he quit paying the rent as soon as he left, and she was evicted. She gave up their child for adoption. If that wasn't bad enough, she showed up at my door pregnant with another man's child. It was a one-night stand; he'd only been in Hawaii on business. She didn't know where he was from or how to let him know she was pregnant with his child. I wanted to help her, but I couldn't. I gave her what little cash I had and told her to go to a women's shelter. I haven't seen my sister since then."

"The timing could have been right for my friend Meredith," Kiana murmured. "She could be your niece."

He shook his head from side to side. "It would be nice to know my sister's kids turned out all right. I never forgave my parents for kicking her out when she was sixteen. They passed several years ago. They never got to know their grandchildren. I never had any of my own—that I know of." He shrugged. "I did have a few girlfriends along the way, but they all ended up marrying other guys."

The man's shoulders sagged.

Dev could sense the older man's sadness.

"It would be a nice surprise to find out I had a son

or daughter," Akana said. "Hell, it'd be nice to know my nieces or nephews. And I'd love to see my sister again to tell her I'm sorry. Will you let me know if your friend is actually my relative?"

Kiana pushed to her feet and dug into her purse. "Meredith would come to see you herself. She'd be beside herself to know she had an uncle or cousin. If you think of anything that might help us find Meredith, would you call me, please?" She handed him her business card. "Thank you for taking time to talk with us."

He looked up at her with sad eyes. "I don't feel like I helped."

"You did," Kiana said.

"Do you think your friend is looking for her mother?" Akana asked. "My sister?"

"We don't know," Kiana said. "Meredith is the only one who can answer that question." She met Dev's gaze. "Ready?"

Dev nodded and held out his hand to steady her as she descended the stairs.

"Miss Williams," Akana called out. "Does your friend look anything like you?"

Kiana's brow wrinkled. "She has dark skin and dark hair like mine. Very much like most native Hawaiians. And she's tall and has green eyes." Kiana smiled. "We get mistaken for sisters."

Akana smiled. "Martina wasn't as tall as you, but she was just as beautiful—only she had brown eyes, not like my green eyes. If you find Martina, tell her I love her and wish her a good and happy life."

"I will," Kiana promised.

Dev led her to the car and opened the door for her.

Kiana sank into her seat and buckled her seatbelt, her gaze on the man who could be Meredith's uncle.

Joe Akana remained in his seat, watching them as Dev backed out of his driveway.

"It breaks my heart," Kiana said softly, "when a family who knows each other and says they love each other falls apart. If I knew my family, I'd fight to keep us together. The world can be a lonely place. Why make it lonelier?"

"Yeah. I was lucky to grow up knowing I was loved by my parents and my siblings, even when we weren't throwing punches at each other. I'd do anything for my brothers and my folks. And they'd do the same."

"You are lucky," she said and sighed. "I don't know what I expected to find here. I think I was hoping Joe would tell us where Meredith was. I know that's ridiculous, but I'd hoped for more of a clue."

"Hopefully, all the pieces we discover will lead us to her."

"Yeah. If only it would lead us there faster. I feel like time is running out." She lifted her chin and turned to him. "Where to from here?"

"I need to have Swede search through birth

records in the state of Hawaii for the timeframe Martina Akana would have had her babies." He handed her his cell phone. "Could you call him?"

"Absolutely." Kiana found the number and clicked on it, setting the cell phone on speaker.

Swede answered on the first ring. "Dev, did you talk with Joe Akana?"

"We did," Dev said. With no idea where to head next, he drove toward Hank and Sadie's Hawaiian vacation home. "I need you to scan Hawaii's Vital Records for any birth certificates listing Martina Akana as the mother."

"Joe's sister?" Swede asked. "On it. Also, I got the name of the man who died by garbage truck."

"Who was he?" Dev asked.

"Timmy Morris," Swede said. "He was known in his gang as 'Spike.'"

Dev's eyes narrowed. "What gang?"

"The one you ran into at The Big Wave," Swede replied. "I spoke with a member of the Honolulu Police Department who has been following gang violence in the city. Apparently, the Order of the Demons is a dangerous gang, pretty much running the city the way they like. Every time one or more of them is brought in on felony charges, they get off with nothing more than a slap on the hand."

"Why?" Kiana asked.

Swede chuckled. "That you, Kiana?"

"Yes, sir," she said. "Why is this gang getting off

without serving time? Are the police and court system afraid of them?"

"My contact in the department says their charges are downgraded before they even get to court. Someone in the department is letting them slide."

"Not good. Especially if these men are after Meredith and now, Kiana," Dev said.

"My contact thinks someone high up is getting kickbacks to cover up their crimes."

Dev shook his head. "If it's that obvious to your contact, you'd think someone would crack down on the corruption in the department."

"My contact was afraid to even talk to me about it," Swede said. "He wasn't just afraid about losing his job. He was afraid for his life and for his family's safety. I suspect he's not the only one on the force afraid to say anything."

"So, this gang is left to do whatever the hell they want with no consequences?" Kiana blew out a breath. "Who has that kind of money and influence to make that happen?"

"Drug cartels? Human traffickers selling girls for big bucks?" Dev suggested. "Criminals who want the police to look the other way and will pay a lot of money to make it happen."

"Who's paying the gang to go after Meredith?" Kiana asked.

Dev's lips pressed into a tight line. "Probably the same person who's paying off the police department."

"Right," Swede said. "Too bad Timmy didn't live long enough for you to interrogate him."

"There are a lot more Timmy's in that gang," Dev pointed out. "Do we need to catch one and beat the truth out of him?"

"I doubt the random gang member would know who's paying them. It would have to be the head honcho, a man who goes by the name Rocko. He's identified as a tattooed badass with spiky white hair. You and Kiana need to steer clear of them. I'll dig more and find the names of the others. If they're getting paid, I might be able to trace the money."

"Assuming they're getting paid via a bank and not in cash under the table," Dev said.

"Right?" Swede said. "Be careful and keep me informed of your next steps. At the very least, keep your backup informed."

"Will do," Dev said. "They came in handy at The Big Wave. Hey, did you find an address for Meredith's boyfriend? We know he worked at The Big Wave, but that's the only information we have. Maybe there's something at his place that will help us locate Meredith." Dev sighed. "We're grasping at straws, I know."

"Actually, I was able to get his address and the phone number for the man in California who was listed as a close relative to Meredith. I'll text both to you. As soon as I get the birth certificates of Martina Akana's babies, I'll get that info to you, as well."

"Thanks. Anything helps," Kiana said.

"I'll get to work on that," Swede said. "Out here."

Kiana ended the call and held his cell phone in her hand. "What next? I feel like we've hit a wall."

A text came through on Dev's phone. Kiana stared down at it. "We have Jason Unger's address. Meredith's ex-boyfriend." She entered it into the map application on Dev's phone. "Guess we'll pay a visit to his apartment. Wouldn't it be great if he was actually there?"

"If he is, he's in danger," Dev pointed out.

"True." She sighed. "It's better than driving around Honolulu aimlessly. We have to find another clue soon. I'll let your guy George know we're headed that way."

"Good." Dev followed the directions to an apartment complex near where Meredith and Tish lived. It didn't look any different than most of the complexes where the city's working people lived. Not the fancy high-rises that housed the tourists with views of the water. This one was tucked into a neighborhood of other complexes, small businesses and some older homes.

After parking in the lot, Dev reached out and caught Kiana's arm before she could open her door. "If *we're* looking here for Meredith, whoever is searching for her will have been here as well and could be watching for her potential return."

Kiana nodded. "Right."

"Stay close and keep your eyes and ears open for anyone lurking in the shadows."

She nodded. "Will do."

Dev had a bad feeling in his gut. He almost aborted the mission to check out Jason's apartment because of that feeling. His hand went to the gun in the holster beneath his lightweight jacket. A firearm was only useful if he saw the threat first. He debated having Kiana wait in the car for him but didn't like the idea of her being out of his sight for even a moment.

Dev got out of the car and rounded the front of the vehicle to open Kiana's door for her.

He liked that she stayed inside the car until he did. After the attacks at Tish's apartment and The Big Wave, she had to be a little more cautious. Most people didn't leave their homes or cars expecting to be jumped by a motorcycle gang. It had to have been eye-opening for Kiana.

He took her hand and helped her out of her seat and onto her feet, tugging a little more than necessary to get her to land in his arms.

"Mmm," she said. "I like this."

"Sweetheart, you have no idea how much I like it, too."

Kiana chuckled. "I have an inkling." She pressed her hips closer to his hardening cock.

"Don't tempt me here. I need to focus." Dev

brushed his lips across hers in a brief kiss. "Have I told you today how much I enjoyed last night?"

"Tell me again," she said with a smile.

His arms tightened around her. "I enjoyed last night."

"Me, too," she said, her smile fading. "Part of me doesn't feel right with how much I liked what happened last night. Especially when Meredith is still missing." She leaned up on her toes and kissed his lips again. "The other part of me was thrilled."

"I have to tell you, at the expense of going against the no-strings promise," he started, "I don't want it to end. We don't have to discuss this now, but I want more time with you." He touched a finger to her lips. "For now, let's find Meredith. We can talk once she's safe."

Kiana stared up into his eyes, kissed the finger still on her lips and nodded. "Okay. Let's see if Jason's home."

They entered the building, climbed the stairs to the second floor and found the apartment number Swede had given them.

Dev knocked on the door. When no one answered, he pressed his ear to the door. "I don't hear anything. I assume he's not home."

"What if he's hiding inside?" Kiana said. "At the least, we need to get inside and see if there are any signs Meredith has been here recently."

"You realize that's breaking and entering," Dev said.

She nodded, digging her hand into her purse. "I like to think it's not breaking if we don't actually break anything. And getting inside is for a good cause." She pulled out a small metal file.

Dev's brow wrinkled. "Do you know how to pick a lock?"

She shrugged. "It made me mad when my foster families locked doors to keep the foster kids out of certain areas of the house. Like we'd steal things. I was curious. I liked knowing what was behind those locked doors." She held up her hands. "I never stole anything. I mean, why risk being kicked out of yet another home? But I could have. I also use my skills at the resort when someone loses a set of keys to a storage room, and we're desperate for more toilet paper. A girl has to do what a girl has to do." She stuck the file into the lock and worked it.

Dev kept watch for anyone entering the hallway.

In less than a minute, he heard the click of a lock being triggered. Kiana twisted the handle and grinned up at him.

He put his hand over hers. "Let me go first."

She nodded and stepped back, letting her hand fall to her side.

Pulling his handgun out of its holster, Dev nudged the door wider and peered through the gap.

When nothing moved inside, he checked the hallway again, then stepped through the doorway.

The apartment appeared like a bachelor pad with a worn leather sofa and an end table made of an old wooden crate with a pizza box lying open on it. The pizza remaining in the box had mold starting to grow on the crust.

Behind him, Kiana entered the apartment and stood just inside, pulling the door closed behind her.

Dev gave her a brief nod and slipped into the only bedroom. The bed was a twist of sheets, and a dark comforter was tossed to one side of the mattress. A chest of drawers stood in one corner, the drawers hanging open as if someone had been in a hurry and hadn't bothered closing them. A closet door stood open with several items of clothing hung inside alongside several empty hangers. A few more hangers lay on the floor again, as if someone had been in a hurry removing clothing from the closet.

There was no one in the bathroom and no sign of shaving gear.

Dev holstered his handgun and returned to the living area, where Kiana waited by the door. "Looks like he left in a hurry."

CHAPTER 11

KIANA WANDERED THROUGH THE APARTMENT, a frown denting her brow. "I don't know what I expected to find."

"See anything belonging to Meredith?" Dev asked.

"Not so far." She entered the bedroom, pushed aside the few items of clothing on the hangers, and then bent to pick up the hangers on the floor. She had them all neatly gathered in her hand when she reached further into the closet and pulled out a pair of hot pink running shoes she recognized.

Kiana straightened. "These are Meredith's old running shoes. She probably left them here at some point."

Dev shook his head. "What do they tell us?"

Kiana's lips twisted. "Only that she's been here at some time. Not where she is now." She sighed. "I don't see anything that will help us."

"Let's go back to Hank and Sadie's, grab something to eat and regroup," Dev said. "Maybe Swede will find something on the internet that will help."

Kiana's shoulders sagged. "There has to be something that will give us a clue. The only thing giving me hope is that the gang came after me."

"Why does that give you hope?"

"If they're trying to grab me, they might want to use me to get to Meredith. Which means they don't have Meredith." Kiana headed for the apartment door. "What I don't understand is why she hasn't called or texted me. Why hasn't she tried to contact me?"

"Maybe she contacted Tish, and that's why she's in the hospital in a coma." Dev stepped in front of Kiana before she could open the door.

She waited while he checked the hallway.

"All clear," he said and held the door for Kiana.

"I wonder if she did try to contact me." Kiana looked up at Dev as she walked past him into the hall. "Remember when we were in the bar, and I got that call from someone who told me to get out?" It didn't sound like her voice, but do you think it could've been Meredith?"

"We should have Swede trace the number." Dev shook his head. "I forgot about that. So much happened so fast after that call, it completely slipped my mind."

"Same." She walked with him to the end of the hall and down the stairs.

Dev stepped out of the building first, checking right and then left. Before he could turn and hold the door for Kiana, a motorcycle roared around the corner of the building, hopped up onto the sidewalk and headed straight for Dev.

Kiana's heart leaped into her throat. She was too far from him to help.

Dev didn't have time to pull his gun. He leaped back, but not far enough.

The man on the bike stuck his foot out and kicked Dev in the chest, sending him flying backward.

Dev hit the wall, the air knocked from his lungs.

The guy ditched his motorcycle, drove past, circled around and came back at Dev.

As he passed the entrance to the building, Kiana came out, screaming like a banshee. She ran at the man and shoved him sideways.

He'd been going so fast that when she shoved him, Kiana spun around.

The man wobbled and fought to regain control.

Dev pushed himself off the wall and lunged for the rider, yanking him off the back of the bike and onto the ground.

The man fell to the ground, landing hard on his back. He rolled over and tried to get up.

Before he could, Dev pounced onto his back, knocking him onto his belly. He grabbed an arm, yanked it up behind the man's back and pinned him. "You need to start talking and fast, or I'll break your goddamn arm."

"Fuck you," the guy said.

Dev pushed the man's arm up high beneath his shoulder blades.

The guy beneath him bucked but couldn't get up.

Kiana hurried over to where Dev had the man pinned to the ground. "Should I call the police?"

The guy snorted. "Yeah. Do that."

"No," Dev said. "Wouldn't do any good. They won't do anything to him. Take my phone from my pocket and text my guys. They'll help me dispose of the body when I'm done with him."

Kiana dug into Dev's jeans pocket for the cell phone, pulled it out and texted George with the address and a message to get there ASAP.

Dev leaned closer to his captive. "After I break your arm, I'm going for your leg. I'll start with the ankle. Then the kneecap. I learned a lot from the Taliban about how to make the pain last."

"You won't get away with it," the man said. "Someone will see you."

"No one gives a rat's ass about you," Dev said. "They'll be glad someone had the balls to take out a member of the gang terrorizing the city." To Kiana, he said. "Grab my gun from my holster, sweetheart."

Kiana shoved his cell phone into her pocket and

did as he asked, reaching beneath his jacket to free the weapon.

"Now, point it at his ankle," Dev said.

"She ain't gonna shoot me," the gang guy said, though he didn't sound quite so sure.

"You willing to bet on that?" Dev said.

"She won't," the man said.

"Kiana?"

Her heart pounding in her chest, she pointed near the man's ankle and pulled the trigger, praying she didn't hit anything.

The sound echoed off the nearby buildings.

"Ha!" the man said. "She missed."

"I wasn't aiming for your ankle," she said in a cool, calm tone. Inside, she was shaking. "Next one won't miss. Where's Meredith Smith?"

"Fuck if I know," he said. "I was told to find her or you and bring one of you back, whatever it took."

"Why?" Kiana asked.

"Fuck if I know," he repeated. "I just follow orders."

"Orders given by who?" Dev asked.

When the man refused to respond, Dev grabbed his hair, pulled back and slammed his face into the concrete.

"Fuck!" the guy cried out as blood spurted from his nose.

"My girl goes for the ankle next. Do you want to start talking? Who gives you orders?" Dev demanded.

"My boss, Rocko," the man said.

"Who gave him his orders?" Kiana asked. "This gun is getting heavy, and my finger is shaking. I might have to aim for something bigger than your ankle." She wasn't lying. The pistol was heavy, and her hand was shaking. "Tell us."

"I don't know!" he yelled. "We don't know his name. He gives Rocko the orders; we carry them out. We never see or hear from him as long as he gets what he wants, and we get what we want."

"So, what's in it for your gang?" Dev asked.

When the gang member didn't respond, Dev pushed the arm he held between the shoulder blades up higher.

The way the guy tensed made Kiana's stomach burble. She feared Dev would make good on his threat to break the man's arm.

The gang member grunted but didn't say anything.

Kiana was so tense her finger tightened on the trigger. The explosion made her jump, and she stared at the man's leg, looking for blood. When she didn't see any, she let go of the breath she'd been holding.

"Damn," Kiana said, feigning nonchalance. "Good thing I wasn't aiming. My finger just squeezed and bang. You might as well talk. We're not letting you loose. My guy's friends will be here in three minutes to dispose of your body."

Where was George? Kiana wasn't sure how much longer Dev could keep the guy down.

"Damn, dude," a breathless voice sounded from behind Kiana. "Who's shooting?"

She spun, aiming her gun at the sound.

George, Rex and another man came running around the corner and ground to a halt when they saw the gun in her hand.

As soon as she recognized them, her cheeks heated. She immediately turned back to their captive.

Dev burst out laughing, the relief evident in the sound. "Glad you made it," he said. "I'll need you to help dispose of the body once we're done with him."

George nodded. "Can do." He turned to Kiana. "Want me to take the gun?"

Dev shook his head. "No. She's got this. Sweetheart, forget the ankle. Go for the knee."

Kiana braced one hand beneath the handgrip and stared down the barrel like she'd seen actors in the movies do, pretending she'd actually fired a gun. "Aiming."

"Fine," the gang member yelled. "I'll tell you. Just get that gun away from her. She's bat-shit crazy."

"I will when you give me something to work with," Dev said. "Until then, she's got her sights set on your knee."

The guy beneath Dev sagged. "You might as well point at my heart or head. If I tell you anything, I'm a dead man."

171

"Dude, then you're screwed," Dev said. "My girl is a former assassin. She always gets her man."

"If I tell you what I know, you have to get me and my family out of here—off the islands, as far from Hawaii as I can get."

"I have friends who can make that happen," Dev said.

"No kidding," the guy said. "Off the island. Me, my girl and my kid. We won't be safe unless we're gone."

"We can do it," George said. "But only if you give us something we need."

"Drugs," the man said. "We do what he wants, and we get drugs, damn it. Enough drugs to sell and make a big enough profit."

"How does that help us find the guy providing them?" Kiana asked.

"I don't know. That's all I have. But there's a delivery tonight. Maybe you can figure it out from there."

"Where is the delivery?" George asked.

"Only Rocko will know the location. The entire gang will be there at midnight. All the Demons will be there. They'll kill anyone who gets in their way."

Dev released the man's arm and stood. He held out a hand and helped the tattooed man to his feet.

George, Rex and Logan formed a circle around the gang member while Dev patted him down, removing his cell phone from his pocket, a knife from his belt and another from his boot. Once he completed his search, he stood back.

"What happens if one of your guys doesn't show up?" Dev asked.

The man stared at the men around him as he wiped his arm across his bloodied nose. "They meet a couple of hours before the designated exchange. If someone is a no-show, they'll find the missing man. If he doesn't have a good excuse for being gone, they'll kill him and his family. That way, everyone shows up. If they don't find the missing man, they call off the exchange until they find him."

Dev nodded. "What's your name?"

The tattooed biker looked around the men surrounding him, his eyes narrowed.

"What's it hurt to tell us now?" Kiana asked. "You said it yourself. You're a dead man."

His lips pressed together for a moment. "Silas," he said. "Silas Miles."

"Silas," Dev patted the man on the back, "guess you'd better make that meeting tonight."

Silas shook his head. "You said you'd get me and my family off the island."

"And we will—after you make that meeting tonight. Since Rocko is the only man who knows where the exchange will take place, we'll need you to lead us to the exchange site."

Silas shook his head. "They'll kill me."

"Only if they know you told them anything," Dev

said. "And the only people who know you told us are those standing around you." He looked at his teammates and Kiana. "Anyone going to tell the Order of the Demons that Silas spilled his guts to us?"

Kiana shook her head, feeling only a little sorry for the man. He would have killed Dev if he'd had half a chance. And he had a reason. A girlfriend and a child? The man probably couldn't get out of the gang even if he wanted to.

Now, he had to lead them to the Order of the Demons so they could follow them to the exchange.

Kiana shivered. It sounded like they were headed into the bowels of hell.

Silas was still shaking his head. "They'll kill me, my girl and kid."

"We'll get your girl and kid out before the meeting," Dev promised. "And we'll get you off the island as soon as we get to the exchange site."

"It'll never work," Silas said. "They'll have lookouts all over the site."

"Not if Rocko is the only man who knows where the exchange takes place."

"Once we meet, Rocko will let us know," Silas said. "We'll move into position and wait for midnight when the drugs will be delivered."

"While the Demons are taking up their positions, we'll move into place."

"You're insane."

Dev's gaze pinned on Silas. "No, we're Marines"

The man's eyes widened. "No shit?"

"He is," George tipped his head toward Dev, then lifted a hand. "So am I."

"Delta Force," Rex said.

"Delta Force," Logan echoed.

"So, you see," Dev said. "Your little gang doesn't scare us. And we don't give two shits about the drugs. We want to find Kiana's friend. If this drug exchange leads us to the man who's dealing it, we'll find our girl."

Silas nodded. "My brother was a Ranger in the Army. He died in Iraq."

"How would he feel if he knew what you were doing?" Kiana asked.

Silas hung his head. "He'd kick my ass." The man lifted his chin. "Get my girl and kid out, and I'll make that meeting."

"Where will we find them?" George asked.

Silas gave him the address.

"You'll understand if we hold onto you until we have them safely away, won't you?" Dev said.

Silas nodded. "I expected that."

George nodded to Rex.

Rex nodded. "We came together in the van."

"Take my rental. It's parked at the side of the building." Dev dug keys out of his pocket and tossed them to Rex.

Rex caught them, left the circle and jogged around the corner of the building.

"In the meantime," Dev said, "let's get out of here before the police follow up on reports that people heard gunfire."

George gripped Silas's arm. "We can take him. I got a van."

"Perfect," Dev said, walking on the other side of Silas. He reached out a hand to Kiana. "I'll take that."

She handed over the pistol, glad to have it off her hands.

Silas ground to a halt. "I can't leave my motorcycle. Someone will steal it."

Logan grinned. "I'll follow on the bike."

"Where are we going?" Kiana asked.

"We rented a small office building not far from here," George said. "We'll hold him there until Rex returns with his family."

"Silas, will your girl and child go with a stranger?"

"If you give me my cell phone, I can call her and let her know," he said.

"Will she be alone?" Dev asked.

"She should be. Sometimes, one of the other girls from the gang stops by to visit."

Dev shook his head and handed Silas his cell phone. "Use my phone. If she's not alone, the other person in the room might wonder why you're calling."

He nodded, took the phone and entered the number.

Kiana worried that Silas would trick them and call his boss, Rocko.

"Hey, babe, don't hang up, it's me," Silas said. "Yeah, I borrowed a buddy's phone. Are you alone?" He paused, listening, his gaze going to Dev. Silas gave a quick nod and continued, "I have a surprise for you and the baby. Pack a diaper bag and an overnight bag for yourself. No, I don't need anything. A friend of mine is going to be by in a few minutes. His name is…"

Dev whispered, "Rex."

"Rex," Silas said into the phone. "He's going to take you and the baby to a surprise destination. I'll meet you there. Yes, you can trust him. No, babe, I'm fine. Just go with him and don't tell anyone you know where you're going. I don't want them to be jealous or anything. Yeah, babe, it'll just be the three of us. See you soon. Love you, too." He ended the call and handed the cell phone to Dev. "She's not buying it."

"Will she go with Rex?" Kiana asked.

"I think so. She's smart and knows that, because I'm a member of the Demons, things can be dangerous between us and other gangs and within the organization. She'll get out."

"Will she tell anyone else?" Kiana asked, worried for Rex.

Silas shook his head. "I told her not to tell. She won't."

"What about her mother, sisters, brothers?" Dev asked.

He gave a tight smile. "We're all the family she has, me and the baby."

"What about your parents or siblings?" George asked.

"My folks and my brother are dead. Lacy and the baby are all the family I have. I used to think the Demons were family, but I've seen them cut members down without batting an eye. When I met Lacy, I'd have left them if I could."

"They don't let you leave unless it's toes up?" Logan guessed as he opened the sliding door of a black van with tinted windows.

"Exactly," Silas climbed into the vehicle, followed by Dev and George.

"Logan will drive," George said.

"Kiana, you can ride back here with us, so no one spots you."

Logan drove the van to the small office building they'd rented for their stay on Oahu. It was an older building in need of paint. Above the office on the ground floor, there appeared to be living quarters.

"This is where we landed when we were assigned to Oahu," George said as they drove around to the back, where there was enough room for four vehicles to park.

Once they were inside the building, Dev left George and Logan with Silas in a small kitchen at the back. He hooked Kiana's arm and walked into the front out of earshot of the others.

"Will George and Logan be able to keep Silas from making a break for it?" she asked, looking over her shoulder.

Dev nodded as he pulled out his cell phone and dialed a number. "They can handle him. I wanted to make a call in private."

"Do you want me to leave?" Kiana started to turn.

He snagged her arm and shook his head as he pressed the phone to his ear. "Hawk, Dev here. We got information from one of the members of the Order of Demons. I don't know how reliable it is, but we're going with it. If it's all he says it is, we'll need a lot more backup."

Dev filled his boss in on what had transpired and what could potentially happen that night. He was asking for help, knowing the night ahead would be dangerous.

As Kiana listened to the one-sided conversation, her pulse quickened. The more time she spent with Dev, the more she wanted. They'd be heading into a dangerous situation that night. Anything could happen. Silas said the gang would kill anyone who got in the way of their drug exchange.

She prayed it wouldn't be Dev.

When Dev got off the phone with Hawk, he appeared as if he felt marginally better. "My boss promised to gather the other men from Kauai and

Maui and bring them to Oahu before nightfall. They'll be geared up and ready to hit the ground running."

"That's good to know," Kiana said.

"I have the communications equipment as well as the weapons Hawk sent with Reid," he said as if ticking items off in his head.

"Now, all we need is for Silas to be telling the truth," Kiana said, "and for him not to spill the beans to the other members of his gang."

"Yeah." Dev's lips twisted. "The last thing we need is to walk into a trap."

"If Silas cares so much about his girl and their baby, he'll do whatever it takes to see to their safety," Kiana pointed out.

Dev nodded. "As long as the Brotherhood Protectors have Lacy and her baby, Silas should do what needs to be done." He glanced at Kiana.

She met his gaze, her brow furrowed. "This all sounds so dangerous," she whispered.

"It is," he said. "When it comes to drugs, there's a lot of money involved. People will kill for that kind of money."

Kiana wrapped her arms around her middle and shivered. "Do we really need to be there for the shipment? Will that shipment give us any idea where to find Meredith?"

Dev had also considered that. "If we can trace the drugs back to the man who shipped them, then yes."

"That's a big *if*," she said. "I'm sure he's put a lot of effort into keeping his identity secret. He hasn't made it easy for the gang to trace, so it won't be easy for anyone else."

He gripped her arms and smiled. "We have Swede. He's the master of tracking things down."

At that moment, Dev's cell phone chirped. He let go of Kiana, pulled his phone out of his pocket and grinned. He tapped to receive the call and then put it on speaker. "Speak of the devil."

Swede laughed. "You wouldn't believe how often I hear that."

"I'd believe you get that a lot." Dev's smile faded. "Just so you know, I'm here with Kiana, and you're on speaker."

"Good. She'll want to hear this," Swede said.

"Tell me what you know," Dev said, "and I'll tell you what we know."

"Deal," Swede said. "I found Martina Akana's children."

Dev frowned. "What do you mean?"

"I found their birth certificates," Swede clarified. "All three of them."

Dev's eyes widened. "Say that again?"

"I found the birth certificates of all three of Martina Akana's children," Swede stated.

"Three?" Kiana's brow dipped. "We only know of two—the one she was pregnant with at sixteen and the one she had three years later."

"There was another six years after the second child."

"Sweet Jesus," Kiana said softly. "Tina M."

"What were the names on the certificates?" Dev asked.

"That's why I called as soon as I had them," Swede said. "I thought the names were interesting."

Kiana leaned forward. "Why?" She held her breath, waiting for his response, a strange feeling washing over her as if whatever Swede had to say would be something that could potentially change her life.

Swede paused for a moment, then answered, "The first baby girl, born thirty-one years ago, was Kiana Samantha Durbin."

CHAPTER 12

DEV'S GAZE shot to Kiana.

She stepped back, her face blanching white beneath her dark skin. "What did you say?"

"Her name was Kiana Samantha Durbin," Swede repeated. "Kiana, did the foster care people give you the name Kiana?"

Kiana shook her head. "No. They told me I knew my first name when I came to them. That I said my name was Kiana, but I didn't know my last name." Her gaze met Dev's.

He went to her, wrapped his arm around her and pulled her close, holding the cell phone out so they could hear what Swede had to say.

"Kiana is a common name in Hawaii," Swede said. "It could be a coincidence that your name and the name on the birth certificate match. Did you say you did a DNA test?"

Kiana nodded.

"She did," Dev said for her. "The results haven't come back yet."

"Wait to get excited until you see those results," Swede advised. "I hate to get your hopes up only for the results to shoot them down."

Kiana swallowed hard, nodding. "Right." She drew in a deep breath. "What were the other names?"

"The second baby girl's name was Bobbi Jo Akana, and the third child, also a girl, was Augustina Ro Akana. She'd be about twenty-two years old now."

"Were any of the fathers named on the birth certificates?" Kiana asked, pressing a shaking hand to her throat.

"Kiana's father was listed as Samuel James Durbin," Swede said. "The other two girls didn't have a father listed. I searched for a Samuel James Durbin in Hawaii, going back for any information I could find around the time baby number one was born. I found a Samuel Durbin assigned to Hickam Air Force Base as a young airman. He was transferred to Eielson Air Force Base in Alaska two years after Kiana's birth. He was killed in a vehicular accident a week after his arrival."

Kiana gasped. "Joe Akana said Martina told him that the father of her first child had left her, saying he'd be back for them. If that father was Samuel Durbin, he couldn't return for them."

"Because he was dead," Swede said.

"They weren't married," Dev added, "and apparently, he hadn't told the military about his child, so they didn't know he had a dependent."

"Martina must've been eighteen by then. She was homeless, with a baby to feed and no job."

"She had to be desperate to give up her child." Dev pressed a kiss to the top of Kiana's head.

"She could've been my mother," Kiana whispered, her voice choking on a sob.

"Like I said," Swede cautioned, "wait for the DNA results. I'm still looking through Meredith's social media. I'll let you know what I find there. Out here."

After Dev ended the call and dropped his cell phone into his pocket, Kiana turned her face into his chest and shook with silent sobs.

Dev held Kiana until she ran out of tears. His shirt was damp, but he didn't care. This woman who'd grown up in foster care, never knowing her mother or where she'd come from, had just been told who her mother and father might have been.

"I'm sorry," she said, pushing away from him.

"For what?" He tipped her chin up.

She laughed, shakily. "I made your shirt wet."

"I don't care." He stared down into her tear-ravaged face. "Are you okay?"

Kiana gave him a watery smile. "I don't need a DNA test to know Martina Akana and Samuel Durbin were my mother and father. And I don't need a DNA test to know Meredith is my sister. I think I knew she was a part of me the moment we met at our foster home all those years ago." She clutched his shirt. "We have to find her. And once we do, we'll find Tina M., our other sister."

"Damn right we will," Dev said and kissed her full on the lips. "And when everyone is back where they belong, I'm going to take you on a date."

She laughed. "Do I get a say in it?"

"Absolutely," he said. "You get to choose where we go."

She leaned her cheek against his chest. "You're on."

"Now, I need to work with my team to come up with a plan. Tonight's mission needs to net information we can use to find Meredith. I don't want to wait much longer for that date. Life's short; we need to seize the day, grab all the happiness we can and hold on tight."

"You're right." Kiana wrapped her arms around his waist and squeezed. "We can't undo the past. Nor should we dwell on it and miss out on embracing the present."

He chuckled and crushed her to him. "I like embracing the present. I plan on doing a lot more of that."

Dev stood for a long moment, loving the way Kiana's arms felt around him. He wanted to get to know her more and to spend time with her when they weren't worried about a friend. To do that, they had to find her friend first.

Not long after Swede's revelation, Rex arrived with Lacy and her baby.

Lacy fell into Silas's arms as soon as she stepped through the door into the back office.

He held her with the baby pressed between them while she told him how she'd packed only enough to get by and not raise suspicion.

Lacy carried a diaper bag with enough diapers for a few days and formula for the same timeframe. She'd stuffed a few items of clothing and toiletries into a backpack, pulled a baseball cap over her hair and met Rex in the driveway when he'd pulled up.

"I didn't know this man named Rex, but the way you sounded on the phone..." She hugged Silas. "I knew I had to go. Rex was kind enough to fit the car seat into his back seat. I pretended we were going to visit friends on the north shore and climbed in like we were old friends." She laughed. "Thankfully, Rex wasn't an axe murderer and did what he said he was going to do, and that was to bring me to you."

Rex chuckled. "She told me she had a knife tucked into her boot and could slit my throat in two seconds flat if I hurt you, her or the baby. I think I was more afraid of her than she was of me."

"I would have cut him," Lacy said, her jaw tight. "I'd cut anyone who hurt my family."

"I know, babe." Silas looked over the top of her head toward Dev. "When will you get them off the island?"

"As soon as my reinforcements arrive," Dev said. "They should be here in the next hour or two."

Silas shook his head. "I feel like we're sitting ducks. What if Rocko gets wind of my defection before you get Lacy and the baby off the island?"

"We'll be okay," Lacy assured him. "Rex promised to take care of us. He's Delta Force. Did you know that?"

Silas smiled down at Lacy. "Yes, I knew that. And if he said he'll take care of you, I'm sure he'll do his best. But you know how many guys are in the Demons and how it's not just the gang watching. There are eyes and ears all over this city. I won't feel like you two are safe until you're off Oahu and on your way to the mainland."

Dev's cell phone dinged with an incoming text. "Our reinforcements are at the airport now. We're to meet them there. It will be harder for any of the Demons to sneak up on us there while we lay out our plans." He nodded to Lacy. "My boss has the plane waiting on standby to take you off the island."

Lacy met Silas's gaze. "Can't you come with us?"

Silas shook his head. "I can't. If I don't show up, they'll come after me and you, no matter where we go. This way, I show up, and everything goes down as usual while you and the baby get away to somewhere you can hide until I can join you at a future date."

Lacy's eyes widened. "Future date? How long will

that be?" She shook her head. "I'm not leaving without you."

"Babe." Silas cupped her chin with a surprising amount of gentleness for a man covered in tattoos who looked like he could chew nails. "I need you two to be safe. Please. Do it for Luke. You said it yourself that you didn't want him to end up in the gang. This is our only chance to make sure he doesn't follow in his dad's footsteps. I don't want him in this mess any more than you do."

She stared up at him for a long moment, frowning fiercely. Finally, she sighed. "Okay. I'll go. But don't do anything stupid and get yourself killed." Her eyes filled with tears. "I love you, you big dumbass."

He smiled. "I love you, too." Then he kissed her.

Dev stood back, giving them a little privacy without leaving them completely alone. He still wasn't sure he could trust Silas. The man could make a dash for freedom at any moment, and they'd miss the opportunity to find the exchange site.

"I moved the baby's car seat into the van," Rex said. "Ready?"

Dev glanced toward Kiana.

She nodded.

Rex, Logan and George surrounded Silas and his small family and marched them out to the black van. Once they were inside with the door closed behind them, Dev and Kiana slid into the rental car. Logan mounted Silas's motorcycle, and they left the office building.

Logan took an alternate route while Dev followed the black van at a safe distance all the way to the airport, where they drove around to the general aviation entrance. They parked outside the designated hangar, and all entered.

Hawk, Angelo Cortez, Teller Osgood, Levi Evans, Jackson Jones and Cord Mendez were all there. How they'd arrived so soon was beyond Dev's comprehension.

Hawk made things happen.

"What a sight for sore eyes." Dev shook hands and hugged the members of his team and the men he'd served with or worked with after they'd left the military. He was glad to see them and to see Hawk. If they ended up taking on the Demons, they'd need all the help they could get.

Hawk crossed to Silas, Lacy and their baby. "They're topping off the fuel on the plane. As soon as they're done, the pilot will file a flight plan to take Lacy and the baby to the mainland. My boss, Hank Patterson, has arranged for them to be taken directly to his ranch in Montana, where they will be safe until you can join them."

Silas stuck out his hand to Hawk. "Thank you. I would've left the Demons a year ago if I could've been certain of Lacy's safety."

"We appreciate that you were willing to let us in

on the plan for the drug exchange," Hawk said. "Lacy and the baby can board the plane now. As soon as they're finished fueling up, they'll leave."

Silas turned to Lacy and pulled her and the baby into his arms. "Know that I love you and little Luke. Whatever happens, keep him safe."

"Nothing's going to happen to you," Lacy insisted. "You're coming to Montana."

"That's right, babe," he said, kissing her and then kissing the baby's cheek. "Take care of your mama, my man." When he raised his head, his jaw firmed. "Now, go."

Lacy's eyes filled, but she gathered the baby close and let Hawk lead her from the hangar to the waiting plane.

Dev laid a hand on Silas's back. "They'll be safe."

"How will they survive if I don't return?" Silas asked, his gaze on Lacy as she climbed the steps up into the plane.

"Hank Patterson and his wife will make sure they're taken care of. You don't have to worry about them." Dev squared his shoulders. "Just focus on getting to the exchange site."

Silas nodded and turned away. "Okay. Tell me what you want me to do."

Once Hawk rejoined them, the men and Kiana gathered in a conference room at one end of the hangar.

"How are you going to follow me to the exchange without being detected by the Demons?" Silas asked.

"We'll send you in with a tracking device," Hawk said. "We'll follow at a safer distance and move in as your guys are establishing a perimeter."

Silas's lips pursed. "Be aware; the Demons won't be the only ones making sure the exchange goes down without a hitch."

Dev's lips thinned. "We understand the Demons operate with immunity when it comes to the Honolulu police."

The big biker nodded. "They will have a presence in the area to keep others out."

"Good to know," Hawk said. "Are there any other organizations protecting the Demons we should know about?"

Silas snorted. "Isn't that enough?"

Hawk's chin rose. "The Brotherhood Protectors consist of men who served as Navy SEALs, Delta Force, Marine Force Recon, Rangers and more. Each man has had multiple deployments to hot zones, fighting enemies much more ruthless than the Demons. I'm not saying we're perfect, but we get the job done, no matter how hard it is or how long it takes."

Silas nodded. "Yeah, but here, you don't always know who is a friend and who is an enemy."

Dev chuckled. "We're very familiar with that scenario."

"Are you going to try to stop the exchange?" Silas asked.

Hawk's brow dipped. "I'm not sure. Even with the men I was able to gather, we won't have enough manpower to bring down the Demons. Right now, let's get you set up with a tracking device. We're giving you one with a panic button. If you're found out, you can hit the button, and we'll have someone there as soon as possible."

Silas's lips pressed together. "Hopefully, before Rocko blows a hole through me or someone else stabs me in the back."

"If you're not okay with doing this, speak now," Hawk said. "We'll send you on that plane with Lacy and Luke."

Dev frowned. If Silas chose to leave at that moment, they didn't have a chance in hell of finding the exchange site.

Silas shook his head. "No. They'll call off the exchange if I don't show up at the designated time and location."

"Is the location and time pre-planned?" Dev asked.

"No," Silas said. "Rocko will text everyone with a special code. I'll need my cell phone for that."

Dev dug Silas's cell phone from his pocket and handed it to him. "I turned it off at the apartment complex in case your gang monitors your location."

Silas nodded. "Good thing you did. I'm sure

Rocko tracks us."

"Will he wonder why your phone is off?" Kiana asked.

He nodded. "I can tell him I forgot to charge it, and it went dead," Silas pocketed the cell phone. "I'll turn it on as soon as I get away from the airport and back closer to the apartment building I was supposed to be watching. I need to get going in case he's already sent out the meeting notice for this evening. You know you can't contact me on my cell phone. I can't risk Rocko getting hold of it."

Dev nodded. "All we need is for you to get to the exchange site just like you usually do. We'll take it from there."

Silas drew in a deep breath and let it out slowly. "Just like usual."

Dev held out his hand. "I know the risk you're taking. Thank you for doing this."

Silas took Dev's hand. "Take care of my family."

"We will." Dev shook the man's hand. He knew he shouldn't, but the look in Silas's eyes made Dev lean toward trusting the man. "Be careful."

"You, too," Silas glanced toward the open bay where he could look out and see the plane containing the woman and child he loved enough to betray the gang.

The engines revved, and the plane rolled slowly out to the taxi lane, picking up speed. Soon, the small jet raced down the runway and lifted off the ground.

"They should be in Montana in six hours," Hawk said. "Hank will meet them at the airport."

Silas nodded, his eyes glassy. Then he turned to Logan.

Logan tipped his head toward the motorcycle he'd parked inside the hangar. "It's all yours."

Silas lifted his chin toward Kiana. "I hope you find your friend." Then he strode toward the motorcycle.

Logan hurried for the door leading out of the hangar and held it open.

Silas drove through and out into the late afternoon sunshine.

"Do you think he'll ditch the tracker?" Kiana asked.

Dev turned to find her standing beside him, her gaze on the door through which Silas had gone.

"If he does, we had Logan tag the motorcycle with another tracker." He slipped his arm around Kiana and pulled her close. "One way or another, we'll find that exchange site."

He turned to his team. "Now that Silas is gone, what's our plan?"

Hawk motioned for the team to gather around. "I notified my contacts on SEAL Team One, stationed at Pearl Harbor. They're gearing up as we speak. They'll move out when we move out and will be tapped into our comms. They promised a ten-man team."

"Are we taking down the gang and the drug

transfer element?" Dev asked.

Hawk nodded. "SEAL Team One will set up on the outer perimeter. We agreed they would provide a contingent to create a distraction that will keep the Honolulu police occupied while our team moves in. The rest of their team will augment ours as we move in." He nodded toward George. "George will man the communications van we'll have parked on the periphery. Everyone else will move in while the Demons set up their perimeter."

In the pause in Hawk's directions, a voice sounded behind Dev. "What about me?"

All gazes turned toward Kiana.

Hawk frowned. "She can stay here in the hangar."

Dev was shaking his head before Hawk finished talking. "We can't leave her unprotected."

"She could ride with me in the van," George said.

Dev frowned. "She's my responsibility. I'll stay back with her."

"George is better at computers and communications. He needs to be in the van," Rex pointed out.

Dev reached for Kiana's hand. "Kiana is *my* assignment."

Kiana squeezed his fingers. "It's all right. I know I can't go with you to the exchange, but maybe I can assist in the communications van. As long as I'm with one of your team, I'll be safe."

Dev's hand tightened around hers. "I'm staying with you."

"We need every man we can muster," Hawk said. "With Reid pulling guard duty at the hospital and George manning the comms van, losing one more to bodyguard duty will knock us down to eight. Even if all ten of the SEAL Team One were available, we'd only have eighteen men against what we estimate to be around thirty-five Demons, and we don't know how many Honolulu police vehicles will be involved.

"You have to go with them," Kiana pleaded. "You know how much this means to me. If it leads us another step closer to Meredith, you know I'd do whatever it takes to make that happen."

Dev didn't like the idea of leaving Kiana, even if he knew George would look out for her.

"I'll be okay," Kiana whispered. "I need you to go with them. Find a clue or someone who knows something to help us find Meredith."

Hawk looked from Dev to Kiana and back to Dev. "It's settled then. Kiana will be in the comms van with George on the periphery, well out of range of the Demons."

Kiana nodded.

Dev didn't like it. Until they found the person responsible for the attacks on Tish and Kiana, he wanted to keep Kiana in his sight at all times. She needed him.

His team needed him, too. It appeared as though he'd been *voluntold* what to do. He'd be on the team going in to secure the exchange site.

CHAPTER 13

WHILE DEV'S TEAM PLANNED, Kiana listened, hanging back to avoid getting in the way. She wanted to know how they would manage to sneak past the Demons to get close enough to the drug delivery without being discovered until it was too late for the gang to do anything about it. It all sounded like an impossible and very dangerous mission.

Kiana's gut knotted at the thought of Dev walking into the middle of the Order of the Demons. Would they shoot anyone they didn't recognize? And what about Silas? Was he to be trusted? Would he let the gang know what was going down and set a trap for the Brotherhood Protectors and the Navy SEAL team?

The team spent the next couple of hours going over all possible scenarios and then distributing communications devices, weapons, ammo and bullet-proof vests. Dev gave Kiana a radio headset. "For you to listen in to what's going on."

He fit it over her head and tested it to ensure it worked, and she knew what to expect.

She was thankful to be allowed to hear what was going on. It made her feel a little like she was included in the mission, though she wouldn't be there physically.

Throughout the day, George monitored Silas's location.

The gang member returned to the apartment complex and remained for an hour. Then, he left, heading for his home address, where Rex had gone to pick up Lacy and the baby.

As the sun descended behind the mountains, Hawk established communications via radio with the contingent from SEAL Team One. When he was satisfied they could communicate clearly, he nodded to his team. "They're ready. It's go time."

The men loaded into the van and other rental vehicles.

Dev would ride in the van with George and some of the others until they were close enough to go the rest of the way on foot.

He slid the door open and helped Kiana up into the van, then climbed in beside her. While the others were filling their vehicles, he looked at Kiana. "Turn around."

She frowned. "Why?"

He gave her a tight smile. "Just do it."

Kiana turned her back to him.

Dev's hands came over her head as he dropped a necklace with a pendant around her neck and hooked it in the back. Then he kissed the nape of her neck. "Just in case we get separated, that's a tracking device. As long as you're wearing it, we can find you."

She spun to face him, her eyes wide. "I'm not planning on getting separated from you or your team."

He cupped her chin and smiled down at her. "You never know what could happen. Just wear it tucked beneath your shirt."

She slid the pendent beneath her blouse, the cold metal chilling her skin at the same time as it warmed her heart. He cared about her, or he wouldn't be worried enough to tag her with a tracking device.

Dev pulled her into his arms and held her as the van navigated the streets of Honolulu, following Silas's tracker.

Kiana was thankful for Dev's strength. He held her up when she was overwhelmed with emotion and nerves.

She really needed to thank Carl for walking out on her and stealing her money. Had he not been such a bastard, Kiana might not have seen Dev for what he was.

A true gentleman. A real man who knew how to treat a woman. Hell, who knew how to treat another person. He cared about her, Meredith and, though he'd pounded on Silas, he'd promised to take care of the man's family.

Kiana bet Dev would look out for Silas at the drug exchange that night, if at all possible. He was a good man. A man she could see herself spending a lot of time with. Maybe even the rest of her life.

Wow. She was getting way ahead of herself.

One step at a time.

First, they had to find Meredith.

"Silas stopped," George said.

Dev's arms stiffened around Kiana. "How far are we from him?"

"Half a mile," Hawk said.

In the van's driver's seat, Logan pulled into a side road and parked against the curb, engine running.

"Rocko will be checking that all the gang showed and then giving them the location of the exchange," Hawk said, his gaze on the screen of the tracking device George held in his hand.

"They still have half an hour before they're due to meet," Dev noted.

"They're moving again," George said, his voice tight.

Hawk spoke into his headset, updating the other Brotherhood Protectors and the group of men from Navy SEAL Team One. "They're moving toward the Port of Honolulu."

When Silas stopped again, Logan pulled the van into an alley half a mile from Silas's location.

The men adjusted their vests, patted their extra magazines of ammunition and double-checked their weapons.

George handed Dev a small handheld tracking device. "It's programmed to give you Silas's location."

Dev nodded and tucked the device into his jacket pocket.

Kiana settled her headset over her ears.

"Game time," Hawk said. "Team BroPro, moving in from the southeast."

"ST1 approaching from the northwest. Spotted one of Honolulu's finest." The SEAL reported the street corner. "Arranging a show for them."

"You heard the man," Hawk said. "It's not just Demons we have to be wary of. Remember, we're not in the sandbox. This isn't Iraq. It's fuckin' Honolulu. If you have to shoot, shoot to wound, if at all possible. Not to kill. Got it?"

The men all nodded and gave a muted, "Yes, sir."

Hawk nodded. "Good. Let's go."

Kiana stood beside the van as the men moved out.

Dev stopped beside her, dropped a kiss on her lips and hurried to catch up to his brothers.

"Kiana," George called out. "We'll monitor from inside the van."

As Dev disappeared into the darkness, Kiana climbed into the van, slid the door closed and settled on the seat next to George, amazed at all the communications equipment the van had been outfitted with.

George gave her a brief explanation of the different devices and how they were used to track each team member.

Though they were far enough to the rear of the conflict, Kiana felt as if she was with them all the way. Her heart pounded, and her breathing grew more rapid. She was terrified for Dev and his team.

At one point, George reached out and laid a hand on her shoulder. "It does no good to get all worked up," he said. "They'll be all right."

She nodded, knowing he was right but still frustrated that she could do nothing to help them.

Kiana listened as the men closed in on the Kahili Container Terminal and Warehouse.

One by one, the teams reported Demon sentinels and Honolulu police units posted at various locations surrounding a particular building.

"A group of Demons just entered a door at the southeast corner of the warehouse," Hawk's voice came through Kiana's headset. "One of the men has a shock of white hair."

Kiana's breath caught in her chest.

"Rocko," Dev's voice sounded in her ear.

Kiana's eyes welled with tears she refused to shed. The men were close enough to identify the man in charge. Close enough to be seen and shot.

"The exchange is about to go down," Dev whispered.

"We could use that distraction about now," Hawk said.

"Team leader ST1," another voice sounded in Kiana's ear. "One distraction coming up."

A moment later, a loud explosion rumbled loud enough that Kiana could hear it inside the van.

"Honolulu's finest moving out to check out the fireworks," a voice said.

"Another on its way to join the fun," said a different voice.

"Three's a charm," another man chimed in.

"Team BroPro moving in," Hawk said.

"ST1 has your six."

Kiana held her breath, listening for any sound. The men went silent as they moved in on the warehouse.

George leaned toward the computer screen with the green dots indicating each man on the team. "Looks like they're inside the warehouse."

"Shots fired," a voice said. "The secret's out. They know we're here."

Kiana pressed a hand to her lips, her chest so tight she could barely breathe.

"Demons moving toward the warehouse from the north. ST1 in position to cut them off."

"Leapfrogging into position. Go, Dev," a voice said.

"Now you, Rex," Dev said.

"Man down!" an excited voice said.

Kiana bit down on her bottom lip to keep from crying out. In the midst of the battle, Kiana's cell phone chirped. She didn't realize it was ringing until it had gone off three times. She jerked her phone out of her pocket and stared down at an unknown number.

Who the hell would be calling her now?

She almost didn't answer when it occurred to her that it might be Silas.

She touched the receive button. "Hello?"

"You have incoming," a familiar female voice said. "Leave. Now!"

"Meredith?" she cried.

"They're almost to you. Go!"

Kiana dove for the driver's seat and fumbled in the dim lighting, looking for the key to turn. "Where the hell is the ignition?"

"What are you doing?" George demanded.

"We have to leave. Now!" She located a start button and mashed it hard with her finger. When the engine roared to life, she let go of the breath she'd been holding, shoved the shift into drive and shot out of the alley as headlights shone in her rearview mirrors.

"How the hell did they find us?" George asked behind her.

"I don't know," Kiana said. "All I *do* know is that

was Meredith who called. She's alive and is looking out for us."

Several plinks sounded against the van's exterior, and then the back, tinted glass shattered.

"They're shooting at us," George called out. "Stay low and go faster."

Kiana slammed her foot to the accelerator, hoping to put distance between her and the people in the vehicle behind her. The people firing live rounds at them.

Her heart stilled when she realized the stop sign ahead indicated a T intersection. She couldn't go straight. She had to go either left or right.

Waiting until the last moment, she shifted her foot from the accelerator to the brake and slammed it down hard, slowing for the turn, knowing it would give the gunmen behind them time to catch up. She had no choice. If she kept going straight, she'd ram into a building.

Left or right?

She spun the steering wheel right. The van turned and kept spinning, performing a three-hundred-sixty-degree circle.

Kiana turned the wheel in the opposite direction, hoping to arrest the spin, but to no avail.

Headlights barreled toward her, and the other vehicle smashed into the passenger side of the van.

Thrown against the driver's door, Kiana's head hit hard. The airbag deployed, and the world went black.

CHAPTER 14

DEV WAS the point man for breaching the building. Rex had his six, with Hawk and Teller behind them.

Bullets hit the ground at his feet as he reached the door, grasped the handle and thanked God that it turned easily.

Not that he'd be any safer stepping inside. He flung open the door and dove to the floor as bullets flew over his head. He rolled toward a forklift and came up into a kneeling position, with the forklift providing cover from the bullets aimed at the door.

He returned fire, forcing the opposing gunmen to duck behind cover, giving Dev's team time to enter the building and take positions behind crates and other machines.

"Comm check," Hawk whispered.

"Rex."

"Teller."

"Dev."

"Hawk," Hawk ended.

Dev was closest to the gunmen. "I spotted a man on top of that stack of crates, three high, to our right. Another directly ahead in a prone position behind the left rear wheel of that pickup."

"I'll distract them," Teller said. "Be ready."

"I'll take the man on the stack," Rex whispered.

"I've got the man behind the wheel," Hawk said.

"And go." Teller left his position and dove behind a row of boxes stacked on wire shelves all the way to the ceiling.

Gunfire erupted from multiple positions.

Dev focused on the shadows moving anywhere else except for those he'd already noted. He picked off a man leaning over the hood of the truck. The man slid to the ground and remained still.

Rex dropped the guy on the stack.

Hawk fired twice, chasing the man behind the truck tire as he attempted to retreat further back.

"You might as well give up. My men are on their way as I speak," a man's voice called out. "You will not leave this warehouse alive unless you surrender now."

"Rocko, your men are surrounded by my men," Hawk responded. "You're the one who won't make it out alive if you don't surrender now."

Rocko chuckled, the sound echoing in the rafters. "A standoff, is it?" The laughter ceased. "So be it."

A man rushed out of the shadows toward Dev's position.

He barely had time to aim and fire. At the last moment, Dev sent a bullet through the guy's chest, dropping him at his feet.

All hell broke loose as Rex leaped forward with Teller covering him. Hawk rushed next. Dev provided cover for his boss and leaped next as the others covered him with a barrage of bullets, keeping Rocko and his guys hunkering low.

Dev saw a flash of white to the right behind a tall row of boxes. "Cover me. I'm going right."

"Got your six," Hawk said. "Go."

Dev circled back a little, clinging to the shadows as he turned and headed toward the row of boxes where he'd seen the flash of white.

He emerged into a row behind his target and spotted Rocko ducking low, peering through the gaps between containers. His handgun was drawn and ready, and one of his men was beside him with a military-grade rifle laid over the top of a box and aimed toward Dev's team.

Dev dropped the man with the rifle and then, before Rocko could turn, shot Rocko in the leg.

The gang leader dropped his pistol and fell to the ground, clutching his thigh.

When Dev emerged from behind the row of boxes, Rocko lunged for his handgun.

Dev kicked it out of the man's reach. "You're

done, Rocko. Your gang is finished terrorizing the city."

Rocko sneered up at Dev. "You're wrong. You may think you have us, but you're so very wrong."

"You probably think your contact on the Honolulu Police Department will let you off again with nothing but a slap on the hand, don't you? I mean, that's what they've done in the past."

Rocko gripped his leg in an attempt to slow the bleeding. He stared up at Dev, his eyes narrow and angry. "You can't touch us."

"I don't have to," Dev said. "You'll bleed out before an ambulance can get here unless I apply a tourniquet."

Rocko's face paled as blood pooled beneath him. "What do you want?"

"I want to know who is supplying your drugs and why you're looking for Meredith Smith."

Rocko swayed and leaned back against the stack of boxes behind him. "I don't know. We do what we're told. We get paid in drugs. I couldn't care less why our benefactor wants this woman as long as he provides us with enough drugs to make a profit on the black market." He stared down at his leg, his expression going from anger to panic. "Fuck. So much blood." He glared up at Dev. "I've told you what I know. Now, stop the bleeding."

Dev stared down at the man who'd given the orders for his men to capture Meredith and Kiana.

He'd read the man's file. He was ruthless and had gotten away with countless murders, with the police turning a blind eye. The man didn't deserve to live.

But Dev wasn't the judge and jury. It wasn't his job to sentence this killer to death, no matter how badly he wanted to.

When Hawk stepped up beside him, he holstered his Glock, unbuckled his belt and knelt beside the leader of the Order of the Demons.

He slipped the belt beneath the man's leg and ran the strap through the buckle, pulling it tight enough to slow the flow of blood.

"I want my belt back," Dev said.

Rocko's eyes rolled back, and he slumped to the side.

As Hawk checked in with the others, Dev pulled the tracking device from his pocket. "I'm going after Silas," he said to Hawk.

"Rex, go with Dev," Hawk ordered.

Dev moved through the shadows, not wanting to risk being shot by a rogue Demon. He was anxious to get back to Kiana. But he couldn't go to her until he was sure Silas was safe.

Moving from one corner of a building to another with Rex covering him, he worked his way toward the green dot on the handheld device. As he approached a large shipping container, he was right where the dot indicated he should find the tattooed gang member.

Crouching in the shadows, he called out softly. "Silas?"

When no one answered, Dev moved toward the end of the shipping container, keeping low and shrouded in darkness. "It's me, Dev," he said just a little louder.

A voice murmured from around the corner of the container. "How do I know you are who you say you are?"

Dev chuckled. "You kicked me in the chest, flying by me on your motorcycle. I can show you the bruise."

Another moment passed, and Silas stepped around the corner of the container. "Is it over?" he asked in a tone barely above a whisper.

"It's over," Dev said. "Let's get you out of here."

"Rocko?"

"I left him passed out in the warehouse. He lost a lot of blood."

"I hope he dies," Silas said.

"You might get your wish," Dev said. He'd done what he could to save the man's life, but the world would be a better place if Rocko didn't make it.

Silas kept his distance. "And the others?"

"Are being rounded up," Rex said.

"Not possible," Silas said. "You were outnumbered at least three to one."

Dev grinned. "We had a little help from some friends."

"What about Lacy and Luke?" Silas lifted his chin.

"Should've landed in Montana by now," Dev said. "Come with me, and we'll call Hank for an update." He was losing his patience with the gang member and was anxious to get back to Kiana.

"Okay. I'll go," Silas said. "But I want off the island on the next flight out."

"Deal." Dev spoke into his headset. "Acquired our informant, headed for the van."

"Roger," Hawk responded. "Wrapping up here. Swede's HPD contact is inbound with reinforcements to process our captives."

Dev frowned. "Will they be released like before?"

"No. One of Rocko's guys offered up the names of the officers taking kickbacks in trade for lighter sentences. We're shutting down the Order of the Demons."

"Good." Dev was happy to hear their efforts wouldn't be in vain. "And the drugs?"

"We have them. Sent images to Swede. He's working to locate the manufacturer."

"Heading to the van now," Dev said.

"Roger," Hawk responded.

As Dev started to walk, Silas shot out a hand to stop him. "Let's take my bike."

Happy to get there faster, Dev followed Silas to where he'd stashed his motorcycle and climbed on behind the big guy.

Dev directed Silas toward the location where

they'd left the van, careful to keep an eye out for trouble. A stray gang member could be lurking in the shadows, ready to get revenge.

"George," Dev said into his mic. "Do you copy?"

George didn't answer. He tried two more times. He'd just spoken to Hawk. Had his mic quit working in that short amount of time? He turned to Rex. "Something must be wrong with my mic. Try raising George."

Rex spoke into his mic, "George, do you copy?"

Again, no response.

Dev frowned. "Kiana? Can you hear me?"

They were getting near to the location.

Silas rounded the corner of the building and entered the alley where they'd left the van.

"Stop!" Dev shouted.

Silas skidded to a halt.

Dev jumped off the back of the motorcycle and stood in an empty alley.

His heart plummeted into his belly.

"You sure this is the right place?" Silas asked, still seated on his bike.

"Yes," Dev said. "Where are they?"

At that moment, his headset erupted in static. "This is George," a voice said that didn't sound at all like the man. "We were…attacked." He drew in a ragged breath as if he was struggling to breathe. "They took…Kiana."

CHAPTER 15

"Kiana."

She heard her name as if it came from the end of a long, dark tunnel.

"Kiana."

Her eyelids were heavy, and pain slashed through her head like a knife. She didn't want to open her eyes. The effort was too much.

"Kiana, please. You have to wake up."

She knew that voice. It pulled her through the darkness into the light.

Kiana opened her eyes and stared up at bright lights glaring down from the ceiling.

Where was she? When she tried to turn her head, the pain sent her back into the black abyss.

"Kiana, please."

The voice penetrated the haze, bringing her back

to the surface. "Meredith." The word emerged as a throaty whisper.

"Yes!" the woman said. "It's me, Meredith. You're awake. Oh, thank God." Her voice trailed off into a sob. "I thought you were dead."

"What happened?" Kiana asked, struggling to push air past her vocal cords.

"They were following you. I couldn't warn you until almost too late."

"That was you," Kiana said, her thoughts fogged with pain. "You called."

"Yes, it was me," Meredith said.

"Where have you been? We've been looking for you?"

"I was hiding."

"Why were you hiding from me and Tish?"

Meredith sighed. "It's a long story."

Kiana tried to raise her hand, but it wouldn't move. Her pulse kicked up. "I remember a crash."

"Yes. They rammed into your van. You must have hit your head."

A terrible thought pushed her closer to clear consciousness. "Am I paralyzed?"

"I don't think so," Meredith said. "You were kicking and flailing when they pulled you out of the van. They wouldn't have strapped you down if you were paralyzed."

Kiana fought through the pain to turn her head and look across the few feet separating them to see her friend lying on a gurney, her arms and legs strapped down. "Why are we strapped to gurneys? What's happening?"

Meredith met Kiana's gaze, tears filling her eyes. "I think I found my sister."

Kiana started to nod her head, but the pain kept her from doing so. Instead, she blinked her eyes. "Tina."

Meredith's eyes rounded. "You know?"

"Found your journal...and logged onto...the ancestry site." Why was it so hard to form sentences? God, her head hurt.

"I was so excited to find relatives. I started a conversation with her on the ancestry site, then we moved to social media messaging and discovered we had so much in common—mannerisms, similar tastes in food, the way we sleep at night. I was so happy to finally find a blood relative. We're not even sure how we're related. Cousins, half-sisters...it doesn't matter. She's family."

"She's your half-sister," Kiana said. "We found birth records for her mother, Martina Akana." She drew in a breath and let it out. "She's your mother, too."

"How do you know?"

"We talked with Joe Akana, the other relative on your ancestry site. He's Martina's brother. Your uncle."

"He's my uncle?" Tears spilled from Meredith's

eyes.

"Your age lines up with the birthdate of one of Martina's three children."

Meredith frowned. "Three children? Who's the other? I only found Tina on the ancestry site."

Kiana hesitated telling Meredith what she suspected. Like Swede said, she needed to wait until the DNA results were in. "Martina Akana had one more, two and a half years before you."

"So, my last name isn't Smith?" Meredith stared up at the lights on the ceiling. "It's Akana."

"And your birth name wasn't Meredith."

She turned toward Kiana. "No?"

Kiana's lips twisted. "You were born Bobbi Jo Akana."

Meredith seemed to chew on that announcement for a moment. "That means Robert Pearson, the other name linked to my DNA, was my father."

"It appears that way. We have the man's phone number. He lives in California, is married, and has two children."

"He's alive?" Meredith shook her head. "All these years, I thought my parents were dead. Why else would I be abandoned as an infant?" She turned to Kiana. "Did you find Martina Akana? Is she alive?"

Kiana shook her head and winced as pain shot through her temple. "There's no record of her current address or place of employment. It's as if she disappeared after giving birth to Tina."

"What about the other child? What was the name on the birth certificate?" Meredith fixed her gaze on Kiana.

Despite their dire predicament, Meredith was still eager to know everything about her blood relatives.

"Last name was Durbin. Her father was listed as a Samuel Durbin. Swede chased the name down to an airman stationed at Hickam at that time. He was transferred to Alaska when the child was two years old. He died in a traffic accident shortly after arriving in Alaska." Kiana said.

"What was the baby's name? I want to find her. I have two sisters."

Kiana still hesitated, not wanting to get Meredith's hopes up any more than her own.

"Tell her," a voice said from across the room. "Tell her the name of the baby on that birth certificate. Martina's oldest child."

A tall man with salt-and-pepper gray hair, wearing a black polo shirt and tailored black slacks, entered the room with one hand in his pocket. "The child's name was Kiana Samantha Durbin."

Meredith's frown deepened.

"Your friend, Kiana Williams, isn't a Williams after all." The man walked slowly toward them, his gaze intense. "She was born Kiana Durbin. She's your half-sister."

Meredith gasped, her gaze shooting to Kiana. "Is that true?"

"I won't know until my DNA results come in."

"Oh, they're in. As of this morning," the man said. "All her life, I thought my precious daughter was an only child. Her mother said she didn't have any other children. I foolishly believed her." He gave a brief, sharp bark of a laugh. "It wasn't until Tina found a close relative through DNA testing that I thought to trace Martina Akana's lineage. Imagine my surprise to find she'd had two other daughters before Tina."

"Who are you?" Kiana asked. "And why are we being held hostage?"

"I'm a man with needs." He turned his back and walked away. "When I married Ingrid, I knew I wanted children. My wife was on board. We tried many times and failed to conceive. After multiple fertility treatments, my wife and I were told we'd never be able to have children." He shook his head.

While the man talked, Kiana worked at the Velcro straps holding her down. No matter how hard she tried, she couldn't break free of them. A captive audience to the insane man, she was forced to listen.

"As an only child," her captor said, "I wanted a houseful of kids. I never thought I couldn't, until..." he shrugged, "I couldn't. I thought it was my wife; she thought it was me. Needless to say, it strained our relationship to the point she lives in New York City, and I live here. In all the years I've lived here, Ingrid has never come to Hawaii. I travel for business and otherwise manage my corporation remotely." He turned to face Kiana and Meredith. "It suits us both."

Kiana almost snorted. She bet it suited him.

"As I said, I'm a man with needs." The man's eyes narrowed. "Twenty-three years ago, I met Martina, a beautiful Hawaiian woman, and took her to my bed for a one-night stand that changed my life forever."

Kiana's stomach roiled.

He turned and walked away again. "That one-night stand resulted in Martina Akana conceiving my child. When she came to me with the news, I accused her of lying. She insisted I was the only man she'd been with in years. I sent her away.

"Nine months later, she showed up at my door with a beautiful baby girl and insisted it was my child. She couldn't afford to raise her. If I didn't take her, she'd have to leave her in foster care. I told her that if a paternity test proved I was the baby's father, I'd keep the child and raise her."

"What does your story have to do with the reason you're holding my sister and me hostage?" Kiana demanded.

The man scowled at Kiana. "I'm getting to that.

"Anyway, the paternity test came back proving I was the father. Because I was married, I couldn't put my name on the birth certificate or publicly claim Tina as my own. Martina wasn't happy with that and wanted me to take her in with the child to make certain she was cared for properly."

Kiana stilled, wanting to hear more about her mother.

"When Martina moved in with Tina, I was beside myself with the joy of being a father. Until I noticed Tina had swelling around her eyes, feet and ankles. More than should be there, even for a chunky baby. And she had a fever we couldn't get under control.

"I had a doctor come to the house to examine her. He recommended I take her to a specialist. The specialist ran tests on that poor baby." The man stared across the room as if seeing into the past. "My beautiful baby girl was in kidney failure."

Kiana's chest tightened at the anguish in the man's tone.

He nodded toward Kiana and Meredith. "Where you and your sister were born healthy and perfect, my darling Tina was not as fortunate. Within a few days of her birth, we were told her kidneys weren't functioning. If she didn't get a kidney transplant, she'd be on dialysis and potentially die before her first birthday."

He pushed a hand through his perfectly combed hair, making it stand on end.

"I have money," he said. "Lots of money, but money alone wouldn't solve the problem. Tina needed a viable kidney from a donor who matched her as closely to perfect as possible. I was tested as a potential donor but wasn't as close of a match as Martina."

"Martina gave Tina a kidney," Meredith filled in.

The man nodded. "She did." He smiled. "Tina flourished, eating and drinking like a normal baby, if a little weaker than most. We homeschooled her to keep her from catching the sickness of the day from other school children."

He drew a deep breath and let it out slowly before continuing his saga. "When she was around thirteen years old, she got so sick we rushed her to the hospital. After all the good years, her body was rejecting her only kidney. It was failing fast. She needed a new one. Martina only had one kidney left, but she wanted Tina to have it. She offered to go on dialysis until a donor kidney could be found to save Tina from having to. The doctors refused to take Martina's kidney and give it to Tina. We were desperate. Martina insisted she wanted to give Tina the kidney. I had the resources, so I brought in everything we'd need here to my home. We set up an operating room, purchased an in-home kidney dialysis machine and flew in the best transplant doctors from other countries."

Kiana's gut clenched. "You performed the transplant here?"

He nodded. "We had everything set up perfectly with all the equipment necessary and the right people to make it happen flawlessly."

Kiana's stomach roiled. The bright overhead

lights, the gurneys, the sterile environment were all making terrible sense now.

"Obviously, the transplant worked. Tina's alive as of the last time we messaged each other," Meredith said.

Tina's father nodded. "Tina came through wonderfully."

"And our mother?" Kiana asked, already knowing the answer.

"They did the best they could." He stared at the wall behind Kiana and Meredith. "She suffered a pulmonary embolism. Nothing they could do could save her. She died that day."

Tears slipped from the corners of Kiana's eyes. She'd never know the mother she'd just found. Ignoring the massive headache, she turned toward Meredith, her sister. They locked gazes, tears flowing.

Meredith's lips pressed into a tight line, and she glared at Tina's father. "In effect, you killed her. How is it you're not in jail? You murdered our mother."

"I saved my daughter," he insisted. "Martina made her choice. She knew the risks."

"There's no record of her death," Kiana said. "We found the birth certificates but no death certificate for Martina Akana."

Tina's father shook his head slowly. "I didn't marry Martina. I still have a wife in New York City whom I never see. Martina lived a good life with no record of her actually living here. We were only lovers once."

"Oh, my God," Meredith cried. "What did you do with her body?"

He straightened his shoulders. "I had her cremated and spread her ashes in the ocean, as per her request."

For a long moment, silence reigned as Kiana and Meredith digested all the man had said.

"Tina mentioned she was unwell," Meredith said quietly. "Is that why we're here?" She said it so resolutely.

Tina's father nodded.

Kiana's chest hurt, her heart breaking for her sisters and herself. She felt sick as full realization sank in. "We're here to provide body parts for your daughter?"

"Your sister," he threw back at her. "She's younger than you and hasn't had a chance to live her life. She deserves the chance to live."

"Did her kidney fail again?" Meredith asked. "You could've asked. We might've offered one of ours without you kidnapping us and stealing parts of our bodies to give to your daughter."

"Does Tina know what you're doing?" Kiana asked. "Is she okay with it?"

"She doesn't know. And she won't. We'll tell her a donor was found. A crash victim or something like that. My baby girl needs a liver this time," he said. "All we're waiting for are the results of tests I'm having run to determine who is the better match. Once I have those results, I have my transplant team on standby."

"Standby, as in they'll fly in from Europe, South America or China?" Kiana asked, praying that was the case, giving them time to figure out how to escape.

"They're here, enjoying a week-long Hawaiian vacation in the villa on my property. I had planned on this being done already. And it would've been done if the Demons hadn't botched the job."

"They were the ones who shot my client and grabbed me out of his car," Meredith said, her voice tired. "They said I couldn't go to the police because I'd be blamed for my client's death. That the police would turn a blind eye toward the Demons." She laughed. "I believed them because I'd seen it happen a number of times. The news would report that they were captured, and then they'd report they'd been released with no charges filed."

"You did that?" Kiana asked. "You're the one who is paying off the Honolulu police? Why?"

"Outfitting an entire operating room and flying in specialists isn't cheap. My pharmaceutical corporation was making money hand over fist for a long time, but we've been hit with a number of lawsuits over the past decade that have drained the coffers and tanked our market shares. The board of directors is focused on the bottom line. I had to come up with another source of income."

"Illegal drug trafficking," Kiana said. "With your own drugs."

"Tina used the name T. Mercer for her social media," Meredith said softly.

"As in Roland Mercer of Mercer Pharmaceuticals?" Kiana curled her lip. "And you're the owner of the corporation, selling your own drugs under the table at a huge profit."

"It pays the bills and keeps my daughter in the medicines she needs so that her body doesn't reject the transplanted organs." His lips pressed into a tight line. "Although, I understand your boyfriend and his friends staged a little coup and captured the leader of the Demons."

That was good news. Hope swelled in Kiana's chest. She prayed Dev hadn't been injured in the process of bringing down Rocko.

"Rocko was getting too careless and cocky. I'll find someone else to do the job," Mercer said. A chirping sound erupted in his pocket. He dug out a cell phone and stared at the screen, a smile curling the corners of his lips. "The results are in." He glanced up, his gaze fixing on Kiana. "Congratulations, Kiana. You're the closest match. You have approximately an hour until the team will be ready. I suggest you say goodbye to your sister."

"No!" Meredith cried. "Don't hurt her. Take me. Tina can have my liver. Leave Kiana out of this."

"Meredith, I'm the logical choice," Kiana said as calmly as she could, though her heart pounded against her ribs. "I'm the closest match."

When Mercer turned to leave the room, Kiana called out, "Mercer, you have me. Let Meredith go. You don't need her. She's not the closest match for Tina. She's of no use to you."

Mercer looked back at Kiana and Meredith, his eyes sad. "You know I can't. She knows too much."

"What are you going to do with her?" Kiana asked.

"Keep her in case my baby needs anything else." He turned and walked toward the door.

"You can't do that," Kiana cried out. "Please. Release her."

"Kiana," Meredith said. "He's not going to let either one of us go free."

"She's right," Mercer said. Neither one of you is getting out of here alive." He left the room, closing the door behind him.

CHAPTER 16

DEV PACED BACK and forth next to what was left of the communications van, sick to his stomach that he hadn't been there to protect Kiana.

After George had announced on the airwaves that Kiana had been taken, Dev brought up her tracking signal on the device he'd used to track Silas. It hadn't taken Dev and Silas long to find the pendant lying on the ground next to the wrecked van.

Dev called 911 immediately. With several ambulances already en route to the warehouse, they diverted one to his location.

Paramedics pulled George from the crushed vehicle and were loading him into an ambulance despite his protests that he was fine.

Dev continued to pace, cursing as he went. "The primary reason we stormed the drug exchange was to get more information about who's behind the deal so we could locate Kiana's friend. Now, we have no more information than we did to start with, and Kiana's missing." He stopped in front of Silas. "Are you absolutely certain you don't know who was supplying the drugs?"

"Sorry, man." Silas shook his head. "I wish I did."

Dev's radio headset crackled in his ears. "Dev, Hawk here. We sent more images of the drugs and their packaging to Swede. He's still working hard to trace the manufacturer. I hope to hear from him soon."

"And how long will it take to trace the shipment back to who authorized it to be sent? If they haven't noticed the missing drugs at the manufacturer by now, it could take weeks to dig through the bullshit to find who sent it here." Dev threw his hands in the air. "Kiana and Meredith might not have weeks."

"Have faith," Hawk urged. "I've seen Swede work miracles before."

Dev stared at the wrecked van, his heart twisting inside his chest. "We could use a miracle right now."

"Hold on, I'm getting a call from Swede now," Hawk said. "I'm making it a three-way call."

Dev's cell phone vibrated in his pocket. He dug it out and answered, "Dev here."

"Are you still there, Swede?" Hawk asked.

"I'm here," Swede's voice came through clearly. "I found a match on the drugs with a manufacturer out of New York. MHP, Inc. the MHP stands for Mercer

Health and Pharmaceuticals. It's a family-owned corporation run by Roland Mercer and his wife, Ingrid."

Dev gripped his phone tightly. "Could you tell who authorized the shipment to be delivered here?"

"Not yet," Swede said.

A heavy weight settled in the pit of Dev's belly. Just as he'd thought, working through a company's shipment authorizations would take time. Time they might not have.

"Something else," Swede continued, "I dug through the ancestry site and found where Tina M gave Meredith her social media name of T. Mercer. It's a bit too much of a coincidence if you ask me."

"Between T. Mercer and Mercer Health and Pharmaceuticals? Yeah. There has to be a connection." Hope welled in Dev's chest. "Were you able to trace the IP address?" His breath caught and held as he waited for Swede's response.

"I did." Swede paused for only a second. "It originated from an address on Oahu. I ran a check on who owns the property at that address. It's owned by ARM Solutions, Inc., a medical research corporation with branches in various countries around the globe. And, get this, it's a subsidiary of MHP, Inc."

"Mercer." Dev's pulse kicked into overdrive. "The address?"

"Sending it via text now," Swede said.

Dev's phone chirped with the incoming text from Swede.

"It might not be the answer," Swede said. "But I hope it helps you find Meredith and Kiana."

"Right now, it's all we have," Dev responded.

"I'm still looking. Anything I find, I'll send your way. Out here." Swede dropped out of the three-way call.

"Hawk, you still there?" Dev asked.

"I am," he replied.

"I'm heading for the address Swede sent."

"How?" Hawk asked. "I thought you said the van was toast."

"Fuck." Dev remembered the fact he'd arrived in the van. He glanced at the wreck. "No one's going anywhere in the van."

"I can have someone pick you up in two minutes," Hawk said.

Silas nudged Dev with his elbow.

Dev glanced at the former gang member. "Hold on, Hawk."

Silas whispered, "Ever ride a motorcycle?"

Dev met Silas's gaze and nodded. "I had one for years as my primary mode of transportation."

Silas gave Dev a tight smile. "Take mine."

"You sure?" Dev asked.

The man nodded. "If it were my girl, I'd already be halfway there."

"Hawk," Dev said, "I'm taking Silas's bike. Meet me at the address Swede gave us. I'll need backup."

"Loading up now," Hawk said. "See you there."

Dev sprinted to Silas's motorcycle with Silas on his heels. He slung his leg over the seat and listened as the biker showed him how to start the machine and shift gears. Thankfully, it was very much like the motorcycle Dev had owned for years.

Silas stood back. "Good luck."

"Thanks." Dev clipped his cell phone into a skeleton-shaped phone holder and brought up the directions to the address Swede had sent. Then he twisted the throttle and sent the motorcycle screaming down the street, praying he'd find Kiana there. If he didn't, he had no idea where else to look.

She had to be there. And if she was, she was probably surrounded by more of the Demons who hadn't been rounded up at the drug exchange.

Hawk would gather as many of the Brotherhood Protectors as he could, along with the SEAL Team One contingent, and be there within minutes of Dev.

Dev weaved through the streets of Honolulu, out onto Highway 1 and then onto the road leading up into Kahili Valley. He turned off the highway onto a paved road that led up a mountain to a massive iron gate. An eight-foot-high concrete block fence stretched in either direction from the gate, disappearing into the jungle. On top of the gate perched a small black camera.

Knowing someone was on the other end of the video surveillance, Dev turned around and headed back the way he'd come as if he was lost and figured he had taken a wrong turn.

As soon as he rounded a curve in the road and was out of sight of the gate and its camera, he pulled off the road, dismounted and waited for the others to catch up. He wouldn't wait long. If they didn't show up quickly, he'd go on without them.

Less than a minute later, several vehicles roared up the road toward him. Dev stepped out of the shadows and waved them down.

Two rental cars and three SUVs pulled to a stop, one behind the other.

Hawk, Rex, Angel and Teller leaped out of the first rental car and joined him. The others gathered around.

Dev explained the gate and fence situation.

"We'll scale the wall out of view of the camera," Dev said. "Assume there will be surveillance equipment and guards inside the walls, positioned throughout the compound."

Not waiting for any further deliberation, he spun on his heel and led the way through the woods to a position further down the fence line, away from the gate and its surveillance camera.

They had no proof Kiana or Meredith were within the walls. If they weren't, they risked being caught and charged with trespassing or, worse, getting shot for trespassing.

Dev was willing to take that risk. If Kiana was inside, he had to get to her. His gut was screaming for him to hurry. One thing he'd learned in all his years in the Marines was that his instinct was never wrong.

CHAPTER 17

"Bullshit," Kiana said between gritted teeth as she lay strapped to the gurney. She refused to be a victim of Mercer's insanity. She had an hour before the transplant would take place. A lot could happen in one hour.

"You heard the man," Kiana said softly. "We have one hour to figure out how to free ourselves from our restraints and get the hell out of Mercer's compound."

"How?" Meredith pulled at the straps securing her arms, wrists, ankles and body to the gurney. "I can't move anything."

Kiana tugged at the straps holding her down, even trying to wiggle her way out from under them, but they were pulled tight.

Desperate to be free, she jerked her body, rocking it back and forth until the gurney wheels banged against the ground. The gurney was heavy-duty, with emphasis on heavy, and designed so that it wouldn't easily flip over. The wheels had been locked to keep it from rolling. It wasn't going anywhere.

"There has to be a way out of this," Kiana said. She leaned her head as far forward as she could, hoping to reach the strap across her chest with the idea of gnawing through it. She wasn't even close.

Then she remembered the pendant Dev had given her with the tracking device. She almost cried when she couldn't feel the pendant where it had nestled between her breasts nor the chain that had secured it around her neck.

Had she lost it in the crash, or had Mercer stripped it off her when he'd brought her into his compound?

She prayed Dev and his team had found the van by now and that they had figured out where she'd been taken. She also prayed for them to do it in less than the hour she and Meredith had left.

"For what it's worth," Meredith said, "we've been sisters even before we knew we were. I love you, Kiana."

"I love you, Meredith. Or should I call you Bobbi Jo?" Kiana forced a laugh. "It would've been nice to get to know our little sister."

Meredith smiled. "From our conversations online, I'd say she has our sense of humor. She sounded like an awesome young woman despite her illness."

Kiana's lips pressed into a tight line. "I'm not ready to give up. I want to get to know Dev better. He promised to take me out on a date. Damn it, I'm going on that date."

"You like him, don't you?" Meredith said.

Kiana nodded. "I do."

"I've been following you. I checked on Tish in the hospital the day she was admitted."

Kiana frowned. "How did you get past Reid?'

Meredith grinned. "I got past you, too." She cocked an eyebrow. "The janitor?"

Kiana's eyes widened. "That was you?"

Meredith nodded. "I was there when the Demons converged on The Big Wave."

"You were the one who told us to get out." Kiana laughed softly. "I should've known."

"I'm sorry I wasn't able to warn you soon enough that time," Meredith said. "I followed the van to where you set up for the drug exchange. I parked my rental car a block away and picked a position where I could watch the road leading up to the building behind which your van was parked. I saw the Demons' SUV coming."

"And you called to warn us." Kiana's heart warmed at her friend's concern. "I recognized your voice that time. I got out of the alley but wasn't fast enough. When I came to the T-intersection, I had to turn one way or the other. I had no choice."

"I know," Meredith said. "I cut through the streets

on foot and was there when the Demons crashed into the van. While they were pulling themselves together, I dragged you free."

"Is that how they caught you?"

"Yeah. You were out cold. A dead weight. I couldn't lift you or drag you fast enough to get you out of sight."

"Meredith, where was Jason? Why wasn't he with you?" Kiana asked.

"Ha," Meredith laid her head back. "I told him someone was after me and might come to him, looking for me. He packed a bag and left for Kauai to stay with some friends there."

Kiana's fists clenched. "He didn't offer to take you with him?"

"Yeah. But I wanted to know who'd killed my client."

"Jason should have stayed with you," Kiana said softly.

"It was easier for me to stay under everyone's radar if I was alone. Jason would have slowed me down," Meredith said. "Besides, I think we were drifting apart."

Kiana snorted. "If he'd given a damn about you and your relationship, he wouldn't have left you."

Meredith sighed. "We were done, anyway."

Kiana's heart hurt for her friend. "Do you know what happened to George, the man in the van with me?"

Meredith shook her head. "The gang was on me before I could get too far. They loaded us into the van they were driving and jabbed a needle into my arm. I never had a chance to look back at the wreckage."

"I hope he's okay." Kiana hoped the entire team had made it through the mission without serious injuries.

Once again, she tried to rock the gurney hard enough to make it turn over.

With the wheels banging against the floor, she didn't hear the door open or close again. It wasn't until a voice said, "Be still," that she realized someone had entered the room.

Kiana lay back against the gurney and stared into the deep brown eyes of a beautiful, ethereal young woman with a thin face and high cheekbones.

"Are you Tina?" she asked.

The young woman smiled. "That's me." Her smile faded as she ripped the Velcro straps off Kiana's wrists. "We need to hurry before they know you're missing." Her thin fingers worked the straps across Kiana's chest, yanking the Velcro apart.

Once Kiana's hands and chest were free, she sat up. A wave of dizziness made her sway. She buried her face in her hands and focused on not passing out. When the dizziness abated, she pulled the straps off her thighs and ankles, then swung her legs over the side of the gurney.

Tina had moved to Meredith and freed her hands and the strap across her chest.

Meredith sat up and flung her arms around Tina. "I can't believe I have not one, but two sisters."

Tina hugged Meredith, tears welling in her eyes. "As soon as I saw your name on the ancestry site, I knew something big was happening." Her narrow shoulders shook. "I always wanted siblings." She looked from Meredith to Kiana. "Now, I have two."

"Soon to be none if your father has his way," Kiana said as she slipped off the gurney onto the floor. Her knees buckled. If she hadn't been holding onto the gurney, she would have fallen in a heap onto the smooth tile floor.

"My father loves me a bit too much," Tina said. "He's too intense. Too controlling."

"He's more than intense," Kiana said. "Do you realize your father wants to harvest our organs for you?"

Tina's face paled. "I heard," she said. "I listened outside the door. I'm so sorry he's done this to you. I would never have agreed to this. This was the first I'd heard that my mother had given me her last kidney. I wouldn't have let her do that if I'd known. They told me she had another, that my first kidney was from a donor." Tears slipped down her cheeks. "She died because of me. You two almost died because of me. I'd rather throw myself off a cliff than have other people die because of me."

Meredith hugged her again. "Nobody needs to die. Let's get out of here, and we'll figure out everything." She released Tina and worked on the straps. Once her ankles were free, she slipped off the gurney and enveloped Tina in a long, hard hug. "I've wanted to do that since our first conversation online. You're amazing."

Tina hugged her back. "I've lived on my father's compound forever. I never knew how great it would feel to be hugged by someone besides him." She grinned at Meredith, who stood a good six inches taller than Tina. "I loved messaging you online. I've never had a real friend."

"Oh, sweetie," Meredith said. "You have us, now."

Tina hugged Meredith once more and then stepped back, shaking her head. "Much as I want to spend more time getting to know my sisters, I need to get you out of here. I won't let my father use you to save me. There has to be another way."

"You should come with us," Kiana said. "We could help you get the medical care you need."

She shook her head. "I've seen so many specialists, been poked and prodded and have taken enough medicines to sink a ship. I can't do it anymore. And I can't let others sacrifice their lives for me." She squared her narrow shoulders. "Come on. You need to go before my father comes back." She hurried for the door.

Kiana crossed to Meredith, hugged her friend—no, her sister—and hurried to follow Tina.

Their younger sibling paused at the door, opening it a crack to peer out into a hallway. "We have to hurry," she whispered. "My father has men guarding the grounds. But I know where there's a gap in the fence you can slip through. I'm not really sure what's on the other side or how you'll get down the mountain, but I know you'll figure it out. Stay close and quiet."

Kiana urged Meredith ahead of her, bringing up the rear. If Tina's plan worked and they managed to escape, they'd have to return and pull the rug out from under Mercer. He couldn't continue to supply illicit drugs to gangs on the islands. People died from drug overdoses every day. Plus, the doctors he'd flown in from all around the world weren't licensed to practice in the States. Roland Mercer was breaking laws with no impunity.

All for the love of his daughter.

How far would Kiana go to save her daughter? Would she break laws to keep a child of hers alive? Would she kill someone to save her child?

She prayed she'd never be placed in that position.

Mercer had protected his daughter to the point of obsession. He'd never let them escape. As wealthy as he was, he was bound to have cameras throughout his home and compound to warn him of intruders, or in this case, of his captives' escape.

Kiana easily kept up with Meredith and Tina.

Their youngest sister didn't move all that fast. With each step, she went a little slower, her frail body barely able to walk very far, much less run. By the time they'd zigzagged through the many corridors to a door leading out into a garden, Tina had to stop to catch her breath.

"Sweetie, are you going to make it?" Meredith slipped an arm around the smaller woman, helped her to a bench and urged her to sit.

"I'm...fine..." Tina said between heaving breaths. "I just...don't...have much...stamina."

While Meredith fussed over Tina, Kiana turned to face the house, expecting men to come rushing out at any moment.

The compound was huge and luxurious. Mercer wouldn't have spared the expense of a security system and someone to monitor it. They'd probably already spotted the escapees and had men on their way to stop them.

"We have to keep moving," Kiana said.

"Yes, we do." Tina pushed to her feet.

Meredith wrapped an arm around Tina's waist, and the two took off down a path leading toward the high wall surrounding the compound.

Kiana followed, looking over her shoulder every other step.

Even if they made it through the fence, they were high up a mountainside with no idea of how far they were from a town. They'd have to get down from that mountain without being recaptured.

At the very least, their escape would buy them a few precious minutes more. Hopefully, enough for Dev and his team to find them.

By the time they reached the back of the tall concrete block fence, Tina was gasping for air. She leaned against the fronds of a stubby palm tree, dragging them to the side to reveal a narrow gap between the blocks. It was wide enough to allow water to drain out of the compound and down the mountainside. If Kiana and Meredith got down on their bellies, they could low-crawl through to the other side.

Kiana waved toward the hole in the wall. "Meredith, you go first. I'll stand guard."

Meredith shook her head. "I'll only go if Tina comes with us."

Tina shook her head. "I can't. If I leave now, I won't have the medicines that help keep me alive."

"We'll get you what you need," Kiana said.

"I don't have a local doctor. They'd want to run more tests. It would take too much time. I don't have...that kind of time." Tina smiled bravely. "I'll be okay. My father wouldn't hurt me."

"Not intentionally," a deep voice said behind Kiana.

Tina spun to face the man standing at the edge of the little clearing. "Dad," she said, pasting an innocent smile on her face. "I was just showing our guests the garden."

Mercer held his jaw so tightly that the muscles on the side of his face twitched with repressed anger. One hand was tucked into his pocket. He waved the other toward the house. "Tina, darling girl, it's late. Our guests need to get back inside. I have a special program all set up for their entertainment."

Tina bent to tie her shoe and came up with a knife in her hand. "No, Dad. I know what you have planned for Meredith and Kiana. I heard what you were saying." When she rose, she flipped open a blade and held it in front of her. "They're my sisters, not my retail store for organs. I won't let you hurt them." She shook her head from side to side, holding the knife out in front of her.

When she swayed a little, Meredith was there to hold her up.

"Tina, step away from these women." Mercer pulled his hand from his pocket along with a small pistol. "I'm only doing what's necessary to save your life."

"If you're killing my sisters to save me, I'd rather die." She shook her head. "Dad, please. Let them go."

"I can't," he said. "You mean everything to me. I can't let you die. I won't." The man aimed the gun at Kiana. "You can come with me willingly, or I'll shoot you and have my men carry you inside."

"No, Dad." Tina stepped between the pistol and

Kiana. "These women are the sisters I always wanted. If I only live another day, I will die happy having spent a little time with them. Please, Dad, don't do this."

Mercer stared at his daughter with such sadness in his eyes that Kiana almost felt sorry for him. "You deserve a life," he said hoarsely.

"Not at the expense of theirs," Tina said, her voice catching on a sob.

"I have to save you." His eyes narrowed. "Now, step aside, Augustina. The doctors are ready."

Tina lifted her chin. "If the only way to keep me alive is to sacrifice one of them..." she drew in a breath and let it go, "then my life isn't worth living." She turned her knife, pressing the tip to her throat. "Let them go, or I'll end this now. I couldn't live with myself, knowing my sister died to save me."

Kiana gasped. "No, Tina. Don't do it."

"Tina." Mercer blanched, and the hand holding the gun shook. "My darling, be reasonable."

His daughter shook her head. "I am. My death is the most reasonable thing I can do. It's the only way to stop this insanity."

CHAPTER 18

ONCE DEV, his team and SEAL Team One reached the fence, Hawk bent over and cupped his hands. "Go!" he said to Dev.

Dev stepped into Hawk's hands and was lifted high enough to hook his arms over the top of the fence. He slung his leg over and straddled the wall.

The others followed suit, helping each other scale the fence.

Dev dropped to the other side and landed inside the manicured grounds of the compound.

The landscaping was carefully designed, with tropical bushes and trees forming trails and pathways throughout what appeared to be several acres of prime mountain real estate.

As soon as Dev hit the ground, he took off running, sticking to the shadows while keeping parallel to the main road leading into the property.

"Keep going, Dev," Hawk said into his headset. "We've got your six."

He found the first sentry several yards from the gate, carrying a military-grade semi-automatic rifle and wearing camouflage combat gear.

Dev eased deeper into the foliage. "One guard beside the main road twenty yards from the gate."

"Got him in our sites. Rex will take him," Hawk said. "Keep moving. We're with you."

Dev moved silently, bypassed the man and resumed forward progress. The trees blocked his view of what lay ahead, but he assumed the buildings would occupy space on high ground to take advantage of whatever view the mountainside offered.

He'd gone at least the length of a football field, steadily climbing, before the bushes and trees thinned and a massive home appeared ahead, perched against the side of a mountain. The modern architecture sported crisp lines of white stucco and huge tinted picture windows.

The beauty of the structure and the surrounding gardens of flowering shrubs and climbing bougainvillea were marred only by the guards patrolling the exterior, carrying the same military-grade rifles as the sentry Dev had passed on the road coming in.

Dev stood in the shadow of a banyan tree with all its many roots trailing from the branches above into the ground below. He spent a moment studying the home's exterior, noting the cameras perched on the corners.

"I'm at your five o'clock," Hawk spoke softly into Dev's headset. "Teller and Levi are circling around to the east."

"Two guards in front," Dev said. "One on the east corner, the other on the west corner. I'll circle around to the west and see if there's a better approach."

"Logan and Jackson will go with you and establish a perimeter," Hawk said.

"Roger." Dev swung wide of the home, clinging to the tree line, staying concealed for as long as possible. It took every bit of his control to keep from rushing the building and demanding to know where they'd taken Kiana.

He could just make out Logan and Jackson behind him. As he continued around, Jackson dropped back to take up a lookout position.

Logan kept pace at a distance, following him to the rear of the building, where a lavish garden with a maze of bushes filled with colorful flowers spread out to the back compound wall. Arched arbors created a fairytale setting that grew all the way out to the tree line where Dev hovered in the shadows.

A voice carried across the garden, barely audible but definitely female.

Dev started forward, ready to race into the garden.

"Hold up, Dev," Logan's voice came through his headset. "Bogey exiting the building on your right."

Dev turned in time to see a man, dressed as the other sentries in camouflage and armed with a rifle, emerge from a door at the corner of the building, heading toward the sound of voices.

Another man emerged and followed the first. Both crouched low, their heads barely above the line of bushes. At a fork in the maze, they split up.

"Once we leave our concealed locations, their surveillance camera will pick up on us. At that point, we're all in," Hawk said.

"Roger," came the response from all the members of the team.

Dev judged the distance he was from the man in the lead. "I've got the man on the left."

"I'll go right," Logan said.

"Going in," Dev said.

"You heard the man," Hawk said. "It's show time."

Dev left the banyan tree, moving quickly and silently across a carpet of grass, entering the maze at a point he'd determined would lead him to his man.

Logan left his concealed position and crossed to the side of the building. He sprinted into the garden, following the same path the two guards had taken when they'd left the building.

As Dev closed in on his guy, his team continued reporting, identifying more guards at different positions around the grounds.

"Sentries on the east side, moving toward the rear of the building," Teller said into the headset. "We'll take them before they reach the corner."

The deeper he ventured into the garden, the more Dev could make out the female voice. He was almost on his guy with one bend in the trail between them when a male voice joined the female's. Then another woman spoke.

Dev's heart flipped.

Kiana.

For a split second, he lost focus and stumbled, making just enough noise to alert the man in front of him. The guard shot a glance over his shoulder. His eyes widened, and Dev shot forward, breaking out into the open near the rear wall where three women stood near a gray-haired man. Dev couldn't be sure, but one of the women held a knife to her own throat.

The guard's partner must have heard the noise and leaped out of the maze at the same time.

"Get the women," the older man called out.

Too far away from his guy, Dev couldn't reach him before he grabbed the woman closest to him.

Sweet Jesus, he had Kiana.

Logan flew out of the bush maze and tackled the other guard. The man hit the ground hard and lay still. Logan leaped to his feet.

Another guard appeared behind him, pointing his rifle at Logan.

"One step closer, and he'll slit Kiana's throat, and

I'll shoot Meredith," the gray-haired man said, aiming his small pistol at the other woman. "Whether they are dead or alive, I'll get what I need."

The man holding Kiana pressed a wicked knife to her throat, holding her in front of him like a shield.

Dev's heart thundered in his chest, but he kept his cool and met the older man's gaze. "It's over, Mercer," he said. "My men outnumber yours. This ends now. Let the women go."

"I can't," Mercer said. "I need them for my baby. Without them, she'll die."

The woman holding the knife to her throat cried out, "No, Daddy, don't do this! Just let me die." She pressed the tip of the blade into her skin and winced. A bead of blood dripped down her neck.

"Tina!" The older man's arm snaked out. He back-handed his daughter, knocking her to the ground. The knife flew from her hand, landing somewhere in the bougainvillea. "Stay out of this," he ordered.

"I won't stay out of this. You're playing God with my life and with theirs." Tina crawled to her knees, tears streaming from her eyes. "If you love me, you won't do this."

"It's because I love you that I have to," he said and spun, aiming his handgun at Dev.

Kiana cried out, "Look out, Dev!"

Dev dove to the right as Mercer's gun went off, the bullet hitting the ground where Dev had been a moment before.

Kiana slammed her head backward into her captor's nose, then swept her arm upward, knocking the hand with the knife away from her throat and dropped all her weight to the ground.

The guard's eyes teared, his nose gushed blood and he lost his hold on Kiana. She rolled out of his reach and back onto her feet.

Meredith threw herself at the guard from behind, sending him toppling to the ground.

Dev rolled to his feet and plowed into Mercer, knocking him onto his back.

Mercer lay still, his eyes closed, out cold.

Dev glanced toward Logan.

"Got this handled," Logan said from where he had the second guard pinned to the ground.

Hawk, Rex, Teller and the rest of his team came around the sides of the house, herding the guards they'd captured.

Dev reached out to help Tina to her feet. "Are you okay?"

She nodded and then shook her head. "No. I'm not okay. I'm so sorry. It's all my fault. As twisted as he was, my father did everything for me. He should've let me die a long time ago, and none of this would have happened."

"I couldn't let you die," Mercer said from where he lay on the ground. "And I won't let you die now." He held his pistol aimed at Kiana.

Tina screamed and threw herself on top of her father.

The gun went off, the sound muffled between their bodies. The father and daughter lay still.

It all happened so fast Dev hadn't had time to react.

"Tina," Kiana cried and rushed toward the young woman.

Dev grabbed her before she reached the pair on the ground, afraid the father still held the gun and would finish what he'd started.

Tina's shoulders shuddered, then she tipped sideways and rolled off her father's body. She landed on her back, her chest covered in blood.

Dev shoved Kiana behind him, placing his body between her and Mercer's gun.

The older man's hand slipped to his side, the gun falling from his grasp to land on the gravel beside him. Though his eyes were wide, his chest didn't move.

"He's dead," Tina said, tears streaming down her cheeks. "I killed him."

"You saved your sisters' lives," Meredith said. Dropping to her knees beside Tina, she gathered the smaller woman into her arms.

Kiana ducked around Dev and knelt by her sisters, wrapping her arms around both. All three women cried.

Dev stood back, finally able to breathe. It was

over. Mercer was dead, Kiana and Meredith were okay, and his job was done.

Hawk came to stand beside him and clapped a hand on his shoulder. "Good job, Mulhaney." He grinned. "Way to nail your first assignment."

"It wasn't just an assignment," Dev said softly.

"No?" Hawk frowned and waved a hand at the women. "You found Meredith and saved your client. I call that a win."

Dev snorted softly. "I did everything my client asked me not to."

"How's that?" Hawk said.

"She said she didn't need a date. I made her promise to go out on a date with me when this was all over. She said she didn't want a relationship. That's all I can think about. She told me not to hit on her." Dev's lips twisted as he recalled making love with Kiana. "That ship has sailed. I wasn't supposed to call her sweetheart. I can't help myself; it just comes out every time I'm near her. And she said not to fall in love with her." He met Hawk's gaze. "Too late. I'm halfway there or more."

Hawk looked from Dev to Kiana and back to Dev. "I know what you mean, man. That's how it happened for me on my first Brotherhood Protectors gig. Kalea blew me away with her strength, loyalty, beauty, kindness and sass. I couldn't help but fall in love with her." He clapped Dev again on the back.

"So, where do you go from here? Are you staying with the Brotherhood?"

Dev nodded. "Damn right. This team is my family." His brow furrowed. "Does it matter what island we live on?"

"Not at all," Hawk said. "Your assignments could take you to any one of them or anywhere in the world, for that matter. Which island will you choose?"

He nodded toward Kiana. "Wherever she lands."

Kiana rose to her feet and crossed to where Dev and Hawk stood. "He forgot one other rule that was broken."

Dev frowned. "I did?"

She gave him a crooked smile. "I said I'm not going to fall in love with you." Kiana leaned up on her toes and brushed her lips across his. "I didn't think it was possible. I thought love was something naïve women thought they needed to validate their existence. I thought I was in love once, even went so far as to get engaged, only to have my fiancé steal my money and dump me."

"Is that what happened with your ex?" Dev's fists tightened. "The bastard didn't deserve you. I'd like to pound him into the ground you walk on."

Kiana laid a hand on Dev's arm. "He did me a favor. He showed me what love wasn't so that when I met you, I'd know what it should be. Now, when are we going on that date you promised me? I want to get to know you better, even though I already know I'm going to love you."

"Let's plan on a day after you get your sister situated. After all, she just lost her father. I think she needs you right now. Don't worry. I'm not going anywhere. I've found the one for me, and I'm not going to let you get away."

EPILOGUE

THREE MONTHS LATER...

"HEY, GORGEOUS." Dev's strong arms wrapped around Kiana and pulled her up against the solid wall of his muscular chest.

"Hey, yourself," she murmured and turned in his arms. "I'm sweaty."

"You're sexy," he said, brushing a damp strand of her hair behind her ear. "You shouldn't be working so hard."

"I'm completely recovered and doing so well you'd never know I gave up half of my liver. I even signed up for a 5K race next month." Kiana grinned. "Tina, Meredith, Tish and I have been training. Tina and Tish will be walking it, but Meredith and I will be running."

"Are you sure it's not too soon for Tish or you?"

"Tish's doctors say she can do anything as long as it's low impact for a while longer. My doctor says my liver is practically back to its normal size. I'm as good as new. Maybe even better since half my liver is newly regenerated." She smiled across at Tina, who was resting in a chair on the lawn next to their Uncle Joe. They'd been laughing over the stories he'd been telling about growing up with their mother. "Look how much color she has in her cheeks. She's beautiful."

Dev didn't shift his gaze from Kiana. "Yes, she is."

Kiana laughed. "You're not even looking at Tina."

"No, I'm looking at the sister I love, thinking how lucky I am to have found you and how I don't want another day to go by without you in my life."

"Even when I smell of sweat and have dirt smeared across my face?"

"Especially when you're sweaty and dirty. You're a smart, capable resort manager. You can stand up for yourself, take down a grown man by breaking his nose and a rib, and you're not afraid of doing grunt work." He brushed his thumb across her cheek. "And you had a big enough heart and the determination to raise the money and bring together all these people to help rebuild your uncle's house. When we're done, it'll be like new and more accessible for his disabilities."

Kiana smiled as she looked at the progress they'd

made in just two days. With the help of the Brotherhood Protectors Hawaii and the SEAL team who'd
helped crack a drug ring and save her life and those
of her sisters, they'd done a lot.

Day one had been demolition day. They'd
cleared Joe's house of all his belongings, sending
much of them to the huge dumpster parked on the
road. The rest they'd stored in a portable storage
box. That same day, they'd gutted Joe's home from
the roof to the floor, taking it down to the studs.
He'd been a little emotional seeing his house
rendered unrecognizable. However, the festive
atmosphere created by the men and women
working together for a cause lifted his spirits, giving
him hope.

Having Tina spend a lot of time getting to know
him had helped even more. She'd enlisted his help
sorting through old photographs to come up with
images they could enlarge to use as artwork for when
they finished the remodel. By the end of the first day,
he'd been smiling and feeling like a contributing
member of the home's transformation.

Today, they'd rewired, replumbed and had all the
drywall hung before noon. While some of the guys
were hanging the drywall inside, another group had
worked on the outside, scraping away flaking paint,
pulling down the old awning and deck, and replacing
them with fresh studs and decking boards. Hawk,
Rex, Logan and George were on the roof. After

rolling out tar paper, they were quickly laying shingles, one after the other, having established a rhythm.

Dev tipped his chin toward the guys on the roof. "They'll have the roof done in the next hour at the rate they're moving."

"Good," Kiana said, turning back to the decking boards stacked in a neat pile. "They can work on the landscaping next while we finish laying in the deck, stairs and ramp." She took a board off the top, laid it across a couple of sawhorses, ran her measuring tape the length of the board and marked where she needed to cut. "Hold that end," she ordered.

While Dev held one end of the board, Kiana cut the other with a circular saw, carried the board to the deck and nailed it in place.

"Perfect fit," Dev said, as he carried another board he'd just cut to lay it beside hers. "Is there no end to your talents, woman?"

"I don't know," she said, sliding into his arms. "You tell me."

"No," he said. "Every day, I discover something new and exciting about you. You continue to acquire new skills."

"I like learning, growing and giving back to my community." She smiled happily.

"Did I tell you that I heard from Silas?" Dev whispered into her ear.

"No, you didn't." She turned and rested her hands

on his chest. "How is he? Does he still like his job as a ranch hand on Hank and Sadie's place?"

Dev chuckled. "He does, though he says riding a horse is a lot more difficult than riding a motorcycle. The horses have minds of their own."

Kiana laughed. "I'm so happy he's making the transition from gang member in Hawaii to ranch hand in Montana."

"Wait until he experiences a winter in Montana. Once he feels minus forty degrees, he might pack up and move back to Hawaii."

"I bet he stays. If not for himself, then for his family. "How are Lacy and Luke?"

"Lacy is working as Sadie's housekeeper and helps with their two children when Sadie's away, working on a film. Luke is learning to walk. He and Sadie's son, McClain, enjoy playing together."

Kiana sighed. "I'm happy for them. I hope they make it back to Oahu someday on vacation. I'd like to see them."

"You don't see them moving back?" Dev asked.

Kiana shook her head. "Why would they? It's expensive living here. Besides, Silas wouldn't risk Lacy and Luke's lives."

"All the gang members have been either jailed or warned that their terrorism days are over. The new police chief isn't going to put up with their shenanigans again. Three strikes and they're out. Most have already had their strikes. They'll end up in jail if they commit another crime."

"Crime has gone down since the assistant police chief was arrested and the officers he used to do his dirty work were fired," Kiana said. "Honolulu is a lot safer place than it was before your team broke up the drug trafficking ring."

"Are you glad you moved back to Oahu?" he asked.

She nodded. "It was nice that the resort I worked for on Maui found me an assistant resort manager position with one of their sister resorts here on Oahu. I get to be closer to my sisters, Meredith, Tina and Tish. It's like we've known each other all our lives. We've become even closer since we had our mother's celebration of life. Uncle Joe was a big help with the preparations."

"Is there any other reason you're glad you moved back to Oahu?" Dev asked, his eyebrows rising up his forehead.

Kiana smiled, leaned up and pressed her lips to his. "Yes. You. It's been a blessing having you live on Oahu instead of going to the Big Island."

Dev sighed. "Agreed. After all that happened in the first few days we were together, I was glad to have time to slow down and get to know you when we weren't fighting for our lives." He held her close.

"Those first few days made me realize a few things I think I knew but had lost sight of."

"Oh, yeah? And what was that?"

She smiled up at him, her heart swelling in her chest, happiness brimming over. "Life's short. I want to experience so much of it with those I love and who love me." She tipped her head toward Meredith and Tish, who were laughing as they pulled on white painter's coveralls. Then she lifted her chin toward Tina, where she sat with Joe, turning the pages of a yellowed photo album and smiling at the pictures. "All my life, I was sad because I had no family. And now, I have three sisters and an uncle. But family isn't only about DNA. It's about the love in your heart." She stared up at Dev. "I'd love all of them, even if we didn't share DNA or a foster home."

"And?" Dev's eyebrows rose hopefully. "Do you have room in your heart for one more?"

Her smile widened. "My heart is so full of my love for them, but that's the thing about love...there's always room in your heart for more."

"Room for someone like...?" he prompted.

Kiana almost laughed at the sad puppy look in his eyes and couldn't help teasing him a little longer. "There's room for someone who makes me want to spend every waking moment with him. Who makes my eggs just the way I like them without being asked. Who makes me want to be the best version of myself, not because he demands it or criticizes me if I'm not, but because he inspires me with his incredible loyalty, bravery, intelligence and kindness."

Dev sighed. "Well, damn. That rules me out."

Kiana flung her arms around his neck. "The hell it does. You're all that and more. Thank you for giving me time to get to know you even better. It just solidified my initial assessment of how I feel about you."

"Cut to the chase, Kiana," he said. "Tell me how you really feel."

"I love you, Devlin Mulhaney, more than I ever knew was possible."

"Grow a pair of balls, Dev," Rex called out from the rooftop.

Kiana laughed as she and Dev looked up to see Rex, Hawk and Logan sitting on the edge of the finished roof.

"That's right," Reid said, stepping out of the house. "Are you going to ask her already, or dick around all day and screw it up?"

George, Levi, Jackson, Angel and Cord came out of the house or from around the sides to stand in a semi-circle, staring at Dev and Kiana expectantly.

Meredith and Tish, dressed in the white painters' jumpsuits and looking like Pillsbury Doughboys, joined the semi-circle along with Tina, Joe and the ST1 team.

Kiana's brow furrowed. "Ask her?" She looked at Dev. "Ask who?"

He stared at her, the smile slipping, his face going straight and serious. "You."

Kiana's heart skipped several beats, and her breathing grew difficult.

"Ask her," Logan chanted. "Ask her. Ask her."

"Ask her," George joined in.

Soon, everyone standing around Kiana and Dev was chanting louder and louder, "Ask her!"

Dev lifted his chin and shouted, "I'm getting to it! Can you all shut up for just a damn minute?"

The group went silent.

Kiana almost laughed at the red stain spreading across Dev's cheeks.

"Do it right, man," Reid said.

"Take a knee," George urged.

"I knew it was a mistake to do this here in front of these yahoos." He gave her a crooked smile. "But the ring came this morning, and I can't wait another minute to know."

He reached into his pocket, pulled out a diamond ring and dropped to one knee.

Kiana's eyes welled.

Dev took her hand in his and looked up into her eyes. "This is the easiest and hardest thing I've ever done in my life."

Kiana shook her head, and her entire body trembled. "Why?"

His gaze dropped to her ringless hand for a moment. "Easiest because I know in my heart you're the best thing to ever happen to me, and I want to be with you always."

Her chest swelled, and tears slipped down her cheeks. "What makes it hard?"

"Knowing that if you don't feel the same, that if you say no, my heart will shatter into a million unrepairable pieces." He stared up into her eyes, his love reflecting in the depths of his gaze. "Please, don't break my heart."

She shook her head. "I wouldn't do that."

His frown deepened. "But you didn't say yes."

"Hey, dipstick," Levi said, "she can't say yes until you ask her the question." He snorted in disgust. "Amateurs."

George shoved Levi. "Like *you've* asked a dozen girls to marry you. Shut up and let the man do it his way." To Dev, he lifted his chin. "Carry on. But make it quick. We want to finish this job sometime today."

"Right," Dev said. "I'm getting there." He cleared his throat. "Before we're interrupted yet again, I'll get to the point." He drew in a breath and let it out. "I love you. I think you love me, and I think we should get hitched. Are you in?"

She laughed and flung herself into his arms. "Yes!"

Dev fell on his ass, pulling Kiana across his lap. "That wasn't nearly as poetic as I'd practiced in the mirror. Nonetheless, the question is legitimate and from my heart. I love you, Kiana, and I can't imagine spending another day without you in my life. Will you marry me?"

She cupped his cheeks between her palms and

smiled into his face. "I already said yes. But I'll say it again, even shout it across the rooftops if you'd like." She drew in a breath and let it out on a sigh. "Yes, Devlin Mulhaney. I love you and want to spend the rest of my life with you. I'm in one-hundred percent."

Dev rose to his feet, drawing her up with him and into his embrace.

Kiana wrapped her arms around him and held him tight, so joyful she felt like her heart would explode. "I've never been happier in my entire life," Kiana said, "than I am right here. With you. Thank you for breaking all my silly rules and for showing me what real love is."

"You heard the lady. She's in!" Dev shouted and spun her around. "She said yes!"

REMY

BAYOU BROTHERHOOD PROTECTORS
BOOK #1

New York Times & USA Today
Bestselling Author

ELLE JAMES

REMY

New York Times & USA Today Bestselling Author
ELLE JAMES

CHAPTER 1

WITH THE SUN dipping over the treetops and dusk settling beneath the boughs of the cypress trees, Deputy Shelby Taylor checked her watch. It would be dark before long. She should be turning around and heading back to the town of Bayou Mambaloa.

Named after the bayou on the edge of which it perched, the town was Shelby's home, where she'd been born and raised. But for a seven-year break, she'd lived in that small town all of her life.

So many young people left Bayou Mambaloa as soon as they turned eighteen. Many went to college or left for employment in New Orleans, Baton Rouge, Houston or some other city. Good-paying jobs were scarce in Bayou Mambaloa unless you were a fishing guide or the owner of a bed and breakfast. The primary industries keeping the town alive were tourism and fishing.

Thankfully, between the two of them, there was enough work for the small town to thrive for at least nine months of the year. The three months of cooler weather gave the residents time to regroup, restock, paint and get ready for the busy part of the year.

As small as Bayou Mambaloa was, it had an inordinate amount of crime per capita. Thus necessitating a sheriff's department and sheriff's deputies, who worked the 911 dispatch calls, responding to everything from rogue alligators in residential pools to drug smuggling.

Shelby sighed. Having grown up on the bayou, she knew her way around on land and in the water.

Her father had always wanted a boy. When all her mother had produced was Shelby and her sister, he hadn't let that slow him down. A fishing guide, her father had taken her out fishing nearly three-hundred-and-sixty-five days of the year, allowing her to steer whatever watercraft he had at the time—pirogues, canoes, bass boats, Jon boats and even an airboat.

Whenever a call came needing someone to get out on the bayou, her name was first on the list. She had to admit that she preferred patrolling in a boat versus in one of the SUVs in the department's fleet. Still, there were so many tributaries, islands, twists and turns in the bayou that if smugglers hid there, they'd be hard to find, even for Shelby.

She'd been on the water since seven o'clock that

morning after an anonymous caller had reported seeing two men on an airboat offloading several wooden crates onto an island in the bayou.

The report came on the heels of a heads-up from a Narcotics Detective with the Louisiana State Police's Criminal Investigations Division.

An informant had said that a drug cartel had set up shop in or near Bayou Mambaloa. The parish Sheriff's Department was to report anything they might find that was suspicious or indicative of drug running in their area.

Because the tip had been anonymous, Sheriff Bergeron had sent Shelby out to investigate and report her findings. She was not to engage, just mark the spot with her GPS and get that information back as soon as possible.

The caller had given a general location, which could have included any number of islands.

Shelby had circled at least ten islands during the day, walked the length of half of them and found nothing.

The only time she'd returned to Marcelle's Marina had been to fill the boat's gas tank and grab a sandwich and more water. At that time, she'd checked in with Sheriff Bergeron. He hadn't had any more calls and hadn't heard from CID. With nothing pressing going on elsewhere in the parish, he'd had Shelby continue her search.

Normally, any chance to get out of the patrol car

and on the water was heaven for Shelby. Not that day. Oppressive, late summer heat bore down on her all day. With humidity at ninety-seven percent, she'd started sweating at eight in the morning, consumed a gallon of water and was completely drenched.

She wished it would go ahead and rain to wash away the stench of her perspiration. Maybe, in the process, the rain would lower the temperature to less than hell's fiery inferno.

She passed a weathered fishing shack and sighed as she read the fading sign painted in blue letters— The Later Gator Fishing Hut. She released the throttle and let the skiff float slowly by.

A rush of memories flooded through her, bringing a sad smile to her lips. Less than a month ago, she'd spent a stormy night in that shack with a man she'd harbored a school-girl crush on for over twenty years.

She'd insisted it would only be a one-night stand they'd both walk away from with no regrets. She didn't regret that night or making love to the man. It had been an amazing night, and the sex had been better than she'd ever dreamed it could be.

However, despite her reassurances to him, she'd come away with one regret.

It had only been one night.

She wanted more.

But that wasn't to be. He'd gone on to the job waiting for him in Montana, never looking back.

He'd left Bayou Mambaloa twenty years ago. His short visit hadn't been enough to bring him back for good.

She hadn't been enough to make him want to stay.

Shelby gave the motor a surge of gas, sending the skiff away from the hut, but her memories followed. Focusing on the waterway ahead, she tried to banish the man and the memories from her thoughts.

By the time she headed back to Marcelle's Marina, the heat had taken its toll. She was tired, cranky and not at her best.

Shelby almost missed the airboat parked in an inlet half-hidden among the drooping boughs of a cypress tree. If movement out of the corner of her eye hadn't caught her attention, she would have driven her boat past without noting the coordinates.

When she turned, she spotted two men climbing aboard an airboat filled with wooden crates.

At the same moment, the taller one of the two men spotted her, grabbed the other man's arm and pointed in her direction.

"Fuck," Shelby muttered and fumbled to capture the coordinates with her cell phone, knowing she wasn't supposed to engage. If these were truly drug smugglers, they would be heavily armed.

The tall man pulled a handgun out of his waistband, aimed at Shelby and fired.

As soon as the gun came out, Shelby ducked.

Though it missed her, the bullet hit the side of her boat.

She dropped her cell phone, hit the throttle and sent the skiff powering through the bayou as fast as the outboard motor would take her.

Another shot rang out over the sound of the engine. The bullet glanced off the top of the motor, cracking the casing, but the engine roared on.

Her heart pounding like a snare drum at a rock concert, Shelby sped through the water, spun around fields of tall marsh grass, hunkering low while hoping she would disappear from their sight long enough to lose herself in the bayou.

For a moment, she dared believe she'd succeeded as she skimmed past a long stretch of marsh grass. She raised her head to peer over the vegetation, looking back in the direction of the two men.

To her immediate right, bright headlights dispelled the dusky darkness as the airboat cleaved a path through the marsh grass, blasting toward her.

Her skiff, with its outboard motor, was no match for the other craft. She had to steer around marsh grass or risk getting her propeller tangled, which meant zig-zagging through the bayou to avoid vegetation.

Not the airboat. Instead of going around, it cut through the field of grass, barreling straight for Shelby in her skiff.

She spun the bow to the left, but not soon enough to avoid the collision.

The larger airboat rammed into the front of the small skiff. The force of the blow launched the skiff into the air.

Shelby was thrown into the water and sank into darkness to the silty floor of the bayou.

As she scrambled to get her bearings and struggled to swim to the surface, the skiff came down hard over her. If not for the water's surface breaking the boat's fall, it would have crushed her and broken her neck. Instead, the hard metal smacked her hard, sending her back down into the silt. Her lungs burned, and her vision blurred.

Her mind numbing, she had only one thought.

Air.

The black water of the bayou dragged at her clothing. The silt at her feet sucked her deeper.

Her head spun, and pain throbbed through her skull. She used every last ounce of strength and consciousness and pushed her booted feet into the silt, sending herself upward. As she surfaced, her head hit something hard, sending her back beneath the water before she could fill her lungs.

Shelby surfaced a second time, her cheek scraping the side of something as she breached the surface and sucked in a deep breath.

She blinked. Were her eyes even open? The darkness was so complete she wondered for a second if the blow making her head throb and her thoughts blur had blinded her. Or was this how it felt to be dead?

She raised her hand to touch the object that had scraped her cheek. Metal. In the back of her mind, she knew she was still in the boat, but it was upside-down. The metal in front of her was the bench she'd been seated on moments before. She wrapped her fingers around the bench to keep her head above water in the air pocket between the bottom of the boat and the bayou's surface.

A whirring sound moved away and then returned, growing louder the closer it came to the inverted skiff. It slowed as it approached. Then metal clanked against metal, and the skiff lurched, the bow dipping lower into the water.

Still holding onto the bench, Shelby's murky brain registered danger. She held on tightly to the bench as the skiff was pushed through the water.

The whir outside increased along with the sound of metal scraping on metal. The front end of the skiff dipped low in the water, dipping the hull lower. Soon, Shelby's head touched the bottom of the boat, and her nose barely cleared the surface.

Whatever was moving the skiff was forcing it deeper.

Shelby had to get out from beneath the boat or drown. Tipping her head back, she breathed in a last breath, released the bench and grabbed for the side of the skiff. She pulled herself toward the edge, ducked beneath it and swam as hard as she could, her efforts jerky, her clothes weighing her down. She couldn't see her hands in front of her, and her lungs screamed for air.

When she thought she couldn't go another inch further, her hands bumped into stalks. She wrapped her fingers around them and pulled herself between them, snaking her way into a forest of reeds. Once her feet bumped against them, she lifted her head above the water and sucked in air. For a moment, the darkness wasn't as dark; the thickening dusk and the glow of headlights gave her just enough light to make out the dark strands of marsh grass surrounding her.

The whirring sound was behind her. Metal-on-metal screeches pierced the air, moving toward her. The grass stalks bent, touching her feet.

In a burst of adrenaline, Shelby ducked beneath the water and threaded her way deeper into the marsh. She moved as fast as she could to get away from the looming hulk of the airboat plowing toward her through the marsh, pushing the skiff beneath it.

The adrenaline and her strength waning, she barely stayed ahead of the skiff being bull-dozed through the grass.

Shelby surfaced for air, so tired she barely had the energy to breathe. It would be so much easier to die.

Holding onto several stalks, she turned to face her death.

The engine cut off. Two lights shined out over the marsh. Another light blinked to life, the beam sweeping over the skiff's hull and the surrounding area.

As the beam neared Shelby, she sank beneath the surface and shifted the reeds enough to cover her head. The beam shone across her position.

Shelby froze. For a long moment, the ray held steady. If it didn't move on soon, she'd be forced to surface to breathe.

When she thought her lungs would burst, the beam shifted past.

Shelby tilted her head back, let her nose and mouth rise to the surface and breathed in.

The light swept back her way so fast she didn't have time to duck lower. Shelby stiffened, her pulse pounding through her veins and throbbing in her head.

Before the light reached her, it snapped off.

She dared to raise her head out of the water enough to clear her ears.

"She has to be dead," a voice said.

Through the reeds, Shelby could just make out two silhouettes between the headlights of the airboat.

"We need to flip the skiff and make sure," a lower voice said.

"I'm not getting in that water to flip no skiff. I saw four alligators earlier."

"You don't see them now," the man with the lower voice argued.

"Exactly why I'm not getting in the water. You don't know where they are in the dark. If you want to check, you get in."

After a pause, the man with the deep voice said. "You're right. Alligators are sneaky bastards."

"Damn right," his partner agreed. "Besides, that woman's dead."

"And if she's not?"

The flashlight blinked on again, the beam directed at the skiff. "She'd better be," the guy with the higher voice said. "Do you see the lettering on the side of that boat?"

"S-h-e-r..." Low-voice man spoke each letter out loud and then paused.

"It spells sheriff," the other guy finished.

"Fuck," low-voice man swore. "We killed a goddamn sheriff?"

"Yeah." The flashlight blinked off. "Let's get the fuck out of here."

The airboat engine revved, and the huge fan on the back of the craft whirred to life. The airboat backed off the skiff and turned, the lights sweeping over Shelby's position.

She sank below the water's surface, the sound of the airboat rumbling in her ears.

Soon, the sound faded.

Shelby bobbed to the surface. The airboat was

gone, and with it, the bright lights. Clouds scudded across the night sky, alternately blocking and revealing a fingernail moon. When it wasn't shrouded in clouds, it glowed softly, turning the inky black into indigo blue.

Her strength waning and her vision fading in and out of a gray mist, Shelby couldn't think past the throbbing in her head.

Out of the haze, the man's comment about alligators surfaced.

She hadn't escaped death by drowning only to become dinner to a hungry reptile.

Somehow, she managed to push her way back through the marsh grass to the mangled hull of the skiff, now crushed low and only a couple of inches above the water's surface. Shelby tried to pull herself up onto the side of the slick metal hull. With nothing to grab hold of, she had no leverage, nor did she have the strength.

Swimming around to the stern, she stepped onto the motionless propeller. With her last ounce of strength and energy, she pushed upward and flopped her body onto the hull. Her forehead bounced against the metal, sending a sharp pain through her already aching head.

Though the clouds chose that moment to clear and let the moon shine down on the bayou, Shelby succumbed to darkness.

ABOUT THE AUTHOR

ELLE JAMES also writing as MYLA JACKSON is a *New York Times* and *USA Today* Bestselling author of books including cowboys, intrigues and paranormal adventures that keep her readers on the edges of their seats. When she's not at her computer, she's traveling, snow skiing, boating, or riding her ATV, dreaming up new stories. Learn more about Elle James at www.ellejames.com

Website | Facebook | Twitter | GoodReads | Newsletter | BookBub | Amazon

Or visit her alter ego Myla Jackson at mylajackson.com
Website | Facebook | Twitter | Newsletter

Follow Me!
www.ellejames.com
ellejamesauthor@gmail.com

ALSO BY ELLE JAMES

Lucas (#3)

Beau (#4)

Rafael (#5)

Valentin (#6)

Landry (#7)

Simon (#8)

Maurice (#9)

Jacques (#10)

Brotherhood Protectors Yellowstone

Saving Kyla (#1)

Saving Chelsea (#2)

Saving Amanda (#3)

Saving Liliana (#4)

Saving Breely (#5)

Saving Savvie (#6)

Saving Jenna (#7)

Saving Peyton (#8)

Saving Londyn (#9)

Brotherhood Protectors Colorado

SEAL Salvation (#1)

Rocky Mountain Rescue (#2)

Ranger Redemption (#3)

Tactical Takeover (#4)

Dog Days of Christmas (#16)

Montana Rescue (#17)

Montana Ranger Returns (#18)

Brotherhood Protectors Boxed Set 1

Brotherhood Protectors Boxed Set 2

Brotherhood Protectors Boxed Set 3

Brotherhood Protectors Boxed Set 4

Brotherhood Protectors Boxed Set 5

Brotherhood Protectors Boxed Set 6

Iron Horse Legacy

Soldier's Duty (#1)

Ranger's Baby (#2)

Marine's Promise (#3)

SEAL's Vow (#4)

Warrior's Resolve (#5)

Drake (#6)

Grimm (#7)

Murdock (#8)

Utah (#9)

Judge (#10)

Delta Force Strong

Ivy's Delta (Delta Force 3 Crossover)

Breaking Silence (#1)

Breaking Rules (#2)

Breaking Away (#3)

Breaking Free (#4)

Breaking Hearts (#5)

Breaking Ties (#6)

Breaking Point (#7)

Breaking Dawn (#8)

Breaking Promises (#9)

Hearts & Heroes Series

Wyatt's War (#1)

Mack's Witness (#2)

Ronin's Return (#3)

Sam's Surrender (#4)

Hellfire Series

Hellfire, Texas (#1)

Justice Burning (#2)

Smoldering Desire (#3)

Hellfire in High Heels (#4)

Playing With Fire (#5)

Up in Flames (#6)

Total Meltdown (#7)

Take No Prisoners Series

The Billionaire Replacement Date (#8) coming soon

The Billionaire Wedding Date (#9) coming soon

Cajun Magic Mystery Series

Voodoo on the Bayou (#1)

Voodoo for Two (#2)

Deja Voodoo (#3)

Cajun Magic Mysteries Books 1-3

The Outriders

Homicide at Whiskey Gulch (#1)

Hideout at Whiskey Gulch (#2)

Held Hostage at Whiskey Gulch (#3)

Setup at Whiskey Gulch (#4)

Missing Witness at Whiskey Gulch (#5)

Cowboy Justice at Whiskey Gulch (#6)

Boys Behaving Badly Anthologies

Rogues (#1)

Blue Collar (#2)

Pirates (#3)

Stranded (#4)

First Responder (#5)

Silver Soldier's (#6)

Warrior's Conquest

Enslaved by the Viking Short Story

Conquests

Smokin' Hot Firemen

Protecting the Colton Bride

Protecting the Colton Bride & Colton's Cowboy Code

Heir to Murder

Secret Service Rescue

High Octane Heroes

Haunted

Engaged with the Boss

Cowboy Brigade

An Unexpected Clue

Under Suspicion, With Child

Texas-Size Secrets